I0617631

The Happiest Time of Their Lives

Alice Duer Miller

1st WORLD
LIBRARY
Literary Society

The Happiest Time of Their Lives

Alice Duer Miller

© 1st World Library – Literary Society, 2004
PO Box 2211
Fairfield, IA 52556
www.1stworldlibrary.org
First Edition

LCCN: 2004195192

Softcover ISBN: 1-4218-0102-7
Hardcover ISBN: 1-4218-0002-0
eBook ISBN: 1-4218-0202-3

Purchase *"The Happiest Time of Their Lives"*
as a traditional bound book at:
www.1stWorldLibrary.org/purchase.asp?ISBN=1-4218-0102-7

1st World Library Literary Society is a nonprofit
organization dedicated to promoting literacy by:

- Creating a free internet library accessible from any
  computer worldwide.
- Hosting writing competitions and offering book
  publishing scholarships.

**Readers interested in supporting literacy
through sponsorship, donations or
membership please contact:
literacy@1stworldlibrary.org
Check us out at: www.1stworldlibrary.ORG
and start downloading free ebooks today.**

The Happiest Time of Their Lives
contributed by Tim, Ed & Rodney
in support of
1st World Library Literary Society

TO CLARENCE DAY, JR.

... and then he added in a less satisfied tone: "But friendship is so uncertain. You don't make any announcement to your friends or vows to each other, unless you're at an age when you cut your initials in the bark of a tree. That's what I'd like to do."

CHAPTER I

Little Miss Severance sat with her hands as cold as ice. The stage of her coming adventure was beautifully set - the conventional stage for the adventure of a young girl, her mother's drawing-room. Her mother had the art of setting stages. The room was not large, - a New York brownstone front in the upper Sixties even though altered as to entrance, and allowed to sprawl backward over yards not originally intended for its use, is not a palace, - but it was a room and not a corridor; you had the comfortable sense of four walls about you when its one small door was once shut. It was filled, perhaps a little too much filled, with objects which seemed to have nothing in common except beauty; but propinquity, propinquity of older date than the house in which they now were, had given them harmony. Nothing in the room was modern except some uncommonly comfortable sofas and chairs, and the pink and yellow roses that stood about in Chinese bowls.

Miss Severance herself was hardly aware of the charm of the room. On the third floor she had her own room, which she liked much better. There was a great deal of bright chintz in it, and maple furniture of a late colonial date, inherited from her mother's family, the Lanleys, and discarded by her mother, who described the taste of that time as "pure, but provincial." Crystal and ivories and carved wood and Italian embroideries did not please Miss Severance half so well as the austere lines of those work-tables and high-boys.

It was after five, almost half-past, and he had said "about five." Miss Severance, impatient to begin the delicious experience of anticipation, had allowed herself to be ready at a quarter before the hour. Not that she had been entirely without some form of anticipation since she woke up; not, perhaps, since she had parted from him under the windy awning the night before. They had held up a long line of restless motors as she stood huddled in her fur-trimmed cloak, and he stamped and jigged to keep warm, bareheaded, in his thin pumps and shining shirt-front, with his shoulders drawn up and his hands in his pockets, while they almost awkwardly arranged this meeting for the next day.

Several times during the preceding evening she had thought he was going to say something of the kind, for they had danced together a great deal; but they had always danced in silence. At the time, with his arm about her, silence had seemed enough; but in separation there is something wonderfully solid and comforting in the memory of a spoken word; it is like a coin in the pocket. And after Miss Severance had bidden him good night at the long glass door of the paneled ball-room without his saying anything of a future meeting, she had gone up-stairs with a heavy heart to find her maid and her wrap. She knew as soon as she reached the dressing-room that she had actually hurried her departure for the sake of the parting; for the hope, as their time together grew short, of having some certainty to look forward to. But he had said nothing, and she had been ashamed to find that she was waiting,

Alice Duer Miller

leaving her hand in his too long; so that at last she snatched it away, and was gone up-stairs in an instant, fearing he might have guessed what was going on in her mind.

She had thought it just an accident that he was in the hall when she came down again, and he hadn't much choice, she said to herself, about helping her into her motor. Then at the very last moment he had asked if he mightn't come and see her the next afternoon. Miss Severance, who was usually sensitive to inconveniencing other people, had not cared at all about the motor behind hers that was tooting its horn or for the elderly lady in feathers and diamonds who was waiting to get into it. She had cared only about arranging the hour and impressing the address upon him. He had given her back the pleasure of her whole evening like a parting gift.

As she drove home she couldn't bring herself to doubt, though she tried to be rational about the whole experience, that it had meant as much to him as it had to her, perhaps more. Her lips curved a little at the thought, and she glanced quickly at her maid to see if the smile had been visible in the glare of the tall, double lamps of Fifth Avenue.

To say she had not slept would be untrue, but she had slept close to the surface of consciousness, as if a bright light were shining somewhere near, and she had waked with the definite knowledge that this light was the certainty of seeing him that very day. The morning had gone very well; she had even forgotten once or twice for a few seconds, and then remembered with a start of joy that was almost painful: but, after lunch, time had begun to drag like the last day of a long sea-voyage.

About three she had gone out with her mother in the motor, with the understanding that she was to be left at home at four; her mother was going on to tea with an elderly relation. Fifth Avenue had seemed unusually crowded even for Fifth Avenue, and the girl had fretted and wondered at the perversity of the police, who held them up just at the moment most promising for slipping through; and why Andrews, the chauffeur, could not see that he would do better by going to Madison Avenue. She did not speak these thoughts aloud, for she had not told her mother, not from any natural love of concealment, but because any announcement of her plans for the afternoon would have made them seem less certain of fulfilment. Perhaps, too, she had felt an unacknowledged fear of certain of her mother's phrases that could delicately puncture delight.

She had been dropped at the house by ten minutes after four, and exactly at a quarter before five she had been in the drawing-room, in her favorite dress, with her best slippers, her hands cold, but her heart warm with the knowledge that he would soon be there.

Only after forty-five minutes of waiting did that faith begin to grow dim. She was too inexperienced in such matters to know that this was the inevitable consequence of being ready too early. She had had time to run through the whole cycle of certainty, eagerness, doubt, and she was now rapidly approaching despair. He was not coming. Perhaps he had never meant to come. Possibly he had merely yielded to a polite impulse; possibly her manner had betrayed her wishes so plainly that a clever, older person, two or three years out of college, had only too clearly read her in

Alice Duer Miller

the moment when she had detained his hand at the door of the ball-room.

There was a ring at the bell. Her heart stood perfectly still, and then began beating with a terrible force, as if it gathered itself into a hard, weighty lump again and again. Several minutes went by, too long for a man to give to taking off his coat. At last she got up and cautiously opened the door; a servant was carrying a striped cardboard box to her mother's room. Miss Severance went back and sat down. She took a long breath; her heart returned to its normal movement.

Yet, for some unexplained reason, the fact that the door-bell had rung once made it more possible that it would ring again, and she began to feel a slight return of confidence.

A servant opened the door, and in the instant before she turned her head she had time to debate the possibility of a visitor having come in without ringing while the messenger with the striped box was going out. But, no; Pringle was alone.

Pringle had been with the family since her mother was a girl, but, like many red-haired men, he retained an appearance of youth. He wanted to know if he should take away the tea.

She knew perfectly why he asked. He liked to have the tea-things put away before he had his own supper and began his arrangements for the family dinner. She felt that the crisis had come.

If she said yes, she knew that her visitor would come just as tea had disappeared. If she said no, she would sit there alone, waiting for another half-hour, and when she finally did ring and tell Pringle he could take away the tea-things, he would look wise and reproachful. Nevertheless, she did say no, and Pringle with admirable self-control, withdrew.

The afternoon seemed very quiet. Miss Severance became aware of all sorts of bells that she had never heard before - other door-bells, telephone-bells in the adjacent houses, loud, hideous bells on motor delivery-wagons, but not her own front door-bell.

Her heart felt like lead. Things would never be the same now. Probably there was some explanation of his not coming, but it could never be really atoned for. The wild romance and confidence in this first visit could never be regained.

And then there was a loud, quick ring at the bell, and at once he was in the room, breathing rapidly, as if he had run up-stairs or even from the corner. She could do nothing but stare at him. She had tried in the last ten minutes to remember what he looked like, and now she was astonished to find how exactly he looked as she remembered him.

To her horror, the change between her late despair and her present joy was so extreme that she wanted to cry. The best she knew how to do was to pucker her face into a smile and to offer him those chilly finger-tips.

He hardly took them, but said, as if announcing a black, but incontrovertible, fact:

"You're not a bit glad to see me."

"Oh, yes, I am," she returned, with an attempt at an easy social manner. "Will you have some tea?"

"But why aren't you glad?"

Miss Severance clasped her hands on the edge of the tea-tray and looked down. She pressed her palms together; she set her teeth, but the muscles in her throat went on contracting; and the heroic struggle was lost.

"I thought you weren't coming," she said, and making no further effort to conceal the fact that her eyes were full of tears she looked straight up at him.

He sat down beside her on the small, low sofa and put his hand on hers.

"But I was perfectly certain to come," he said very gently, "because, you see, I think I love you."

"Do you think I love you?" she asked, seeking information.

"I can't tell," he answered. "Your being sorry I did not come doesn't prove anything. We'll see. You're so wonderfully young, my dear!"

"I don't think eighteen is so young. My mother was married before she was twenty."

He sat silent for a few seconds, and she felt his hand shut more firmly on hers. Then he got up, and, pulling a chair to the opposite side of the table, said briskly:

"And now give me some tea. I haven't had any lunch."

"Oh, why not?" She blew her nose, tucked away her handkerchief, and began her operations on the tea-tray.

"I work very hard," he returned. "You don't know what at, do you? I'm a statistician."

"What's that?"

"I make reports on properties, on financial ventures, for the firm I'm with, Benson & Honaton. They're brokers. When they are asked to underwrite a scheme - "

"Underwrite? I never heard that word."

The boy laughed.

"You'll hear it a good many times if our acquaintance continues." Then more gravely, but quite parenthetically, he added: "If a firm puts up money for a business, they want to know all about it, of course. I tell them. I've just been doing a report this afternoon, a wonder; it's what made me late. Shall I tell you about it?"

She nodded with the same eagerness with which ten years before she might have answered an inquiry as to whether he should tell her a fairy-story.

"Well, it was on a coal-mine in Pennsylvania. I'm afraid my report is going to be a disappointment to the firm. The mine's good, a sound, rich vein, and the labor conditions aren't bad; but there's one fatal defect - a car shortage on the only railroad that reaches it. They can't make a penny on their old mine until that's met, and that can't be straightened out for a year, anyhow; and so I shall report against it."

"Car shortage," said Miss Severance. "I never should have thought of that. I think you must be wonderful."

He laughed.

"I wish the firm thought so," he said. "In a way they do; they pay attention to what I say, but they give me an awfully small salary. In fact," he added briskly, "I have almost no money at all." There was a pause, and he went on, "I suppose you know that when I was sitting beside you just now I wanted most terribly to kiss you."

"Oh, no!"

"Oh, no? Oh, yes. I wanted to, but I didn't. Don't worry. I won't for a long time, perhaps never."

"Never?" said Miss Severance, and she smiled.

"I said *perhaps* never. You can't tell. Life turns up some awfully queer tricks now and then. Last night, for example. I walked into that ballroom thinking of nothing, and there you were - all the rest of the room like a sort of shrine for you. I said to a man I was with, 'I want to meet the girl who looks like cream in a gold saucer,' and he introduced us. What could be stranger than that? Not, as a matter of fact, that I ever thought love at first sight impossible, as so many people do."

"But if you don't know the very first thing about a person - " Miss Severance began, but he interrupted:

"You have to begin some time. Every pair of lovers

have to have a first meeting, and those who fall in love at once are just that much further ahead." He smiled. "I don't even know your first name."

It seemed miraculous good fortune to have a first name.

"Mathilde."

"Mathilde," he repeated in a lower tone, and his eyes shone extraordinarily.

Both of them took some time to recover from the intensity of this moment. She wanted to ask him his, but foreseeing that she would immediately be required to use it, and feeling unequal to such an adventure, she decided it would be wiser to wait. It was he who presently went on:

"Isn't it strange to know so little about each other? I rather like it. It's so mad - like opening a chest of buried treasure. You don't know what's going to be in it, but you know it's certain to be rare and desirable. What do you do, Mathilde? Live here with your father and mother?"

She sat looking at him. The truth was that she found everything he said so unexpected and thrilling that now and then she lost all sense of being expected to answer.

"Oh, yes," she said, suddenly remembering. "I live here with my mother and stepfather. My mother has married again. She is Mrs. Vincent Farron."

"Didn't I tell you life played strange tricks?" he exclaimed. He sprang up, and took a position on the hearth-rug. "I know all about him. I once reported on the Electric Equipment Company. That's the same Farron, isn't it? I believe that that company is the most efficient for its size in this country, in the world, perhaps. And Farron is your stepfather! He must be a wonder."

"Yes, I think he is."

"You don't like him?"

"I like him very much. I don't *love* him."

"The poor devil!"

"I don't believe he wants people to love him. It would bore him. No, that's not quite just. He's kind, wonderfully kind, but he has no little pleasantnesses. He says things in a very quiet way that make you feel he's laughing at you, though he never does laugh. He said to me this morning at breakfast, 'Well, Mathilde, was it a marvelous party?' That made me feel as if I used the word 'marvelous' all the time, not a bit as if he really wanted to know whether I had enjoyed myself last night."

"And did you?"

She gave him a rapid smile and went on:

"Now, my grandfather, my mother's father - his name is Lanley - (Mr. Lanley evidently was not in active business, for it was plain that Wayne, searching his memory, found nothing) - my grandfather often scolds me terribly for my English, - says I talk like a barmaid, although I tell him he ought not to know how barmaids talk, - but he never makes me feel small. Sometimes Mr. Farron repeats, weeks afterward, something I've said, word for word, the way I said it. It makes it sound so foolish. I'd rather he said straight out that he thought I was a goose."

"Perhaps you wouldn't if he did."

"I like people to be human. Mr. Farron's not human."

"Doesn't your mother think so?"

"Mama thinks he's perfect."

"How long have they been married?"

"Ages! Five years!"

"And they're just as much in love?"

Miss Severance looked at him.

"In love?" she said. "At their age?" He laughed at her, and she added: "I don't mean they are not fond of each other, but Mr. Farron must be forty-five. What I mean by love - " she hesitated.

"Don't stop."

But she did stop, for her quick ears told her that some one was coming, and, Pringle opening the door, Mrs. Farron came in.

She was a very beautiful person. In her hat and veil, lit by the friendly light of her own drawing-room, she seemed so young as to be actually girlish, except that she was too stately and finished for such a word. Mathilde did not inherit her blondness from her mother. Mrs. Farron's hair was a dark brown, with a shade of red in it where it curved behind her ears. She had the white skin that often goes with such hair, and a high, delicate color in her cheeks. Her eyebrows were fine and excessively dark - penciled, many people thought.

"Mama, this is Mr. Wayne," said Mathilde. Here was another tremendous moment crowding upon her - the introduction of her beautiful mother to this new friend, but even more, the introduction to her mother of this wonderful new friend, whose flavor of romance and interest no one, she supposed, could miss. Yet Mrs. Farron seemed to be taking it all very calmly, greeting him, taking his chair as being a trifle more comfortable than the others, trying to cover the doubt in her own mind whether she ought to recognize him as an old acquaintance. Was he new or one of the ones she had seen a dozen times before?

There was nothing exactly artificial in Mrs. Farron's manner, but, like a great singer who has learned perfect enunciation even in the most trivial sentences of every-day matters, she, as a great beauty, had learned the perfection of self-presentation, which probably did not wholly desert her even in the dentist's chair.

She drew off her long, pale, spotless gloves.

"No tea, my dear," she said. "I've just had it," she added to Wayne, "with an old aunt of mine. Aunt Alberta," she threw over her shoulder to Mathilde. "I am very unfortunate, Mr. Wayne; this town is full of my relations, tucked away in forgotten oases, and I'm their only connection with the vulgar, modern world. My aunt's favorite excitement is disapproving of me. She was particularly trying to-day." Mrs. Farron seemed to debate whether or not it would be tiresome to go thoroughly into the problem of Aunt Alberta, and to decide that it would; for she said, with an abrupt change, "Were you at this party last night that Mathilde enjoyed so much?"

"Yes," said Wayne. "Why weren't you?"

"I wasn't asked. It isn't the fashion to ask mothers and daughters to the same parties any more. We dance so much better than they do." She leaned over, and rang the little enamel bell that dangled at the arm of her daughter's sofa. "You can't imagine, Mr. Wayne, how much better I dance than Mathilde."

"I hope it needn't be left to the imagination."

"Oh, I'm not sure. That was the subject of Aunt Alberta's talk this afternoon - my still dancing. She says she put on caps at thirty-five." Mrs. Farron ran her eyebrows whimsically together and looked up at her daughter's visitor.

Mathilde was immensely grateful to her mother for taking so much trouble to be charming; only now she rather spoiled it by interrupting Wayne in the midst of a sentence, as if she had never been as much interested as she had seemed. Pringle had appeared in answer to her ring, and she asked him sharply:

"Is Mr. Farron in?"

"Mr. Farron's in his room, Madam."

At this she appeared to give her attention wholly back to Wayne, but Mathilde knew that she was really busy composing an escape. She seemed to settle back, to encourage her visitor to talk indefinitely; but when the moment came for her to answer, she rose to her feet in the midst of her sentence, and, still talking, wandered to the door and disappeared.

As the door shut firmly behind her Wayne said, as if there had been no interruption:

"It was love you were speaking of, you know."

"But don't you think my mother is marvelous?" she asked, not content to take up even the absorbing topic until this other matter had received due attention.

"I should say so! But one isn't, of course, overwhelmed to find that your mother is beautiful."

"And she's so good!" Mathilde went on. "She's always thinking of things to do for me and my grandfather and Mr. Farron and all these old, old relations. She went away just now only because she knows that as soon as Mr. Farron comes in he asks for her. She's perfect to every one."

He came and sat down beside her again.

"It's going to be much easier for her daughter," he said: "you have to be perfect only to one person. Now, what was it you were going to say about love?"

Again they looked at each other; again Miss Severance had the sensation of drowning, of being submerged in some strange elixir.

She was rescued by Pringle's opening the door and announcing:

"Mr. Lanley."

Wayne stood up.

"I suppose I must go," he said.

"No, no," she returned a little wildly, and added, as if this were the reason why she opposed his departure. "This is my grandfather. You must see him."

Wayne sat down again, in the chair on the other side of the tea-table.

CHAPTER II

Mathilde had been wrong in telling Wayne that her mother had gone upstairs in obedience to an impulse of kindness. She had gone to quiet a small, gnawing anxiety that had been with her all the day, a haunting, elusive, persistent impression that something was wrong between her and her husband.

All the day, as she had gone about from one thing to another, her mind had been diligently seeking in some event of the outside world an explanation of a slight obscuration of his spirit; but her heart, more egotistical, had stoutly insisted that the cause must lie in her. Did he love her less? Was she losing her charm for him? Were five years the limit of a human relation like theirs? Was she to watch the dying down of his flame, and try to shelter and fan it back to life as she had seen so many other women do?

Or was the trouble only that she had done something to wound his aloof and sensitive spirit, seldom aloof to her? Their intimate life had never been a calm one. Farron's interests were concentrated, and his temperament was jealous. A woman couldn't, as Adelaide sometimes had occasion to say to herself, keep men from making love to her; she did not always want to. Farron could be relentless, and she was not without a certain contemptuous obstinacy. Yet such conflicts as these she had learned not to dread, but sometimes deliberately to precipitate, for they ended always in a deeper sense of unity, and, on her part, in a fresh sense of his supremacy.

If he had been like most of the men she knew, she would have assumed that something had gone wrong in business. With her first husband she had always been able to read in his face as he entered the house the full history of his business day. Sometimes she had felt that there was something insulting in the promptness of her inquiry, "Has anything gone wrong, Joe?" But Severance had never appeared to feel the insult; only as time went on, had grown more and more ready, as her interest became more and more lackadaisical, to pour out the troubles and, much more rarely, the joys of his day. One of the things she secretly admired most about Farron was his independence of her in such matters. No half-contemptuous question would elicit confidence from him, so that she had come to think it a great honor if by any chance he did drop her a hint as to the mood that his day's work had occasioned. But for the most part he was unaffected by such matters. Newspaper attacks and business successes did not seem to reach the area where he suffered or rejoiced. They were to be dealt with or ignored, but they could neither shadow or elate him.

So that not only egotism, but experience, bade her look to her own conduct for some explanation of the chilly little mist that had been between them for twenty-four hours.

As soon as the drawing-room door closed behind her she ran up-stairs like a girl. There was no light in his study, and she went on into his bedroom. He was lying on the sofa; he had taken off his coat, and his arms were clasped under his head; he was smoking a long cigar. To find him idle was unusual. His was not a contemplative nature; a trade journal or a detective novel were the customary solace of odd moments like this.

He did not move as she entered, but he turned his eyes slowly and seriously upon her. His eyes were black. He was a very dark man, with a smooth, brown skin and thick, fine hair, which clung closely to his broad, rather massive head. He was clean shaven, so that, as Adelaide loved to remember a friend of his had once suggested, his business competitors might take note of the stern lines of his mouth and chin.

She came in quickly, and shut the door behind her, and then dropping on her knees beside him, she laid her head against his heart. He put out his hand, touched her face, and said:

"Take off this veil."

The taking off of Adelaide's veil was not a process to be accomplished ill-advisedly or lightly. Lucie, her maid, had put it on, with much gathering together and looking into the glass over her mistress's shoulder, and it was held in place with shining pins and hair-pins. She lifted her head, sank back upon her heels, and raised her arms to the offending cobweb of black meshes, while her husband went on in a tone not absolutely denuded of reproach:

"You've been in some time."

"Yes," - she stuck the first pin into the upholstery of

the sofa, - "but Pringle told me Mathilde had a visitor, and I thought it was my duty to stop and be a little parental."

"A young man?"

"Yes. I forget his name - just like all these young men nowadays, alert and a little too much at his ease, but amusing in his way. He said, among other things - "

But Farron, it appeared, was not exclusively interested in the words of Mathilde's visitor; for at this instant, perceiving that his wife had disengaged herself from her veil, he sat up, caught her to him, and pressed his lips to hers.

"O Adelaide!" he said, and it seemed to her he spoke with a sort of agony.

She held him away from her.

"Vincent, what is it?" she asked.

"What is what?"

"Is anything wrong?"

"Between us?"

Oh, she knew that method of his, to lead her on to make definite statements about impressions of which nothing definite could be accurately said.

"No, I won't be pinned down," she said; "but I feel it, the way a rheumatic feels it, when the wind goes into the east."

He continued to look at her gravely; she thought he was going to speak when a knock came at the door. It was Pringle announcing the visit of Mr. Lanley.

Adelaide rose slowly to her feet, and, walking to her husband's dressing-table, repinned her hat, and caught up the little stray locks which grew in deep, sharp points at the back of her head.

"You'll come down, too?" she said.

Farron was looking about for his coat, and as he put it on he observed dryly:

"The young man is seeing all the family."

"Oh, he won't mind," she answered. "He probably hasn't the slightest wish to see Mathilde alone. They both struck me as sorry when I left them; they were running down. You can't imagine, Vin, how little romance there is among all these young people."

"They leave it to us," he answered. This was exactly in his accustomed manner, and as they went down-stairs together her heart felt lighter, though the long, black, shiny pin stuck harmlessly into the upholstery of the sofa was like a mile-stone, for afterward she remembered that her questions had gone unanswered.

Wayne was still in the drawing-room, and Mathilde, who loved her grandfather, was making a gentle fuss over him, a process which consisted largely in saying: "O Grandfather! Oh, you didn't! O *Grandfather*!"

Mr. Lanley, though a small man and now over sixty, had a distinct presence. He wore excellent gray clothes of the same shade as his hair, and out of this neutrality of tint his bright, brown eyes sparkled piercingly.

He had begun life with the assumption that to be a New York Lanley was in itself enough, a comfortable creed in which many of his relations had obscurely lived and died. But before he was graduated from Columbia College he began to doubt whether the profession of being an aristocrat in a democracy was a man's job. At no time in his life did he deny the value of birth and breeding; but he came to regard them as a responsibility solemn and often irritating to those who did not possess them, though he was no longer content with the current views of his family that they were a sufficient attainment in themselves.

He was graduated from college in 1873, and after a summer at the family place on the Hudson, hot, fertile, and inaccessible, which his sister Alberta was at that time occupying, he had arranged a trip round the world. September of that year brought the great panic, and swept away many larger and solider fortunes than the Lanleys'. Mr. Lanley decided that he must go to work, though he abandoned his traditions no further than to study law. His ancestors, like many of the aristocrats of the early days, had allowed their opinions of fashion to influence too much their selection of real estate. All through the late seventies, while his brothers and sisters were clinging sentimentally to brownstone fronts in Stuyvesant Square or red-brick facades in Great Jones Street, Mr. Lanley himself, unaffected by recollections of Uncle Joel's death or grandma's marriage, had been parting with his share in such properties, and investing along the east side of the park.

By the time he was forty he was once more a fairly

rich man. He had left the practice of law to become the president of the Peter Stuyvesant Trust Company, for which he had been counsel. After fifteen years he had retired from this, too, and had become, what he insisted nature had always intended him to be, a gentleman of leisure. He retained a directorship in the trust company, was a trustee of his university, and was a thorny and inquiring member of many charitable boards.

He prided himself on having emancipated himself from the ideas of his own generation. It bored him to listen to his cousins lamenting the vulgarities of modern life, the lack of elegance in present-day English, or to hear them explain as they borrowed money from him the sort of thing a gentleman could or could not do for a living. But on the subject of what a lady might do he still held fixed and unalterable notions; nor did he ever find it tiresome to hear his own daughter expound the axioms of this subject with a finality he had taught her in her youth. Having freed himself from fine-gentle-manism, he had quite unconsciously fallen the more easily a prey to fine-ladyism; all his conservatism had gone into that, as a man, forced to give up his garden, might cherish one lovely potted plant.

At a time when private schools were beginning to flourish once more he had been careful to educate Adelaide entirely at home with governesses. Every summer he took her abroad, and showed her, and talked with her about, books, pictures, and buildings; he inoculated her with such fundamentals as that a lady never wears imitation lace on her underclothes, and the past of the verb to "eat" is pronounced to rhyme with "bet." She spoke French and German fluently, and could read Italian. He considered her a perfectly educated woman. She knew nothing of business, political economy, politics, or science. He himself had never been deeply interested in American politics, though very familiar with the lives of English statesmen. He was a great reader of memoirs and of the novels of Disraeli and Trollope. Of late he had taken to motoring.

He kissed his daughter and nodded - a real New York nod - to his son-in-law.

"I've come to tell you, Adelaide," he began.

"Such a thing!" murmured Mathilde, shaking her golden head above the cup of tea she was making for him, making in just the way he liked; for she was a little person who remembered people's tastes.

"I thought you'd rather hear it than read it in the papers."

"Goodness, Papa, you talk as if you had been getting married!"

"No." Mr. Lanley hesitated, and looked up at her brightly. "No; but I think I did have a proposal the other day."

"From Mrs. Baxter?" asked Adelaide. This was almost war. Mrs. Baxter was a regal and possessive widow from Baltimore whose long and regular visits to Mr. Lanley had once occasioned his family some alarm, though time had now given them a certain institutional safety.

Her father was not flurried by the reference.

"No," he said; "though she writes me, I'm glad to say, that she is coming soon."

"You don't tell me!" said Adelaide. The cream of the winter season was usually the time Mrs. Baxter selected for her visit.

Her father did not notice her.

"If Mrs. Baxter should ever propose to me," he went on thoughtfully, "I shouldn't refuse. I don't think I should have the - "

"The chance?" said his daughter.

"I was going to say the fortitude. But this," he went on, "was an elderly cousin, who expressed a wish to come and be my housekeeper. Perhaps matrimony was not intended. Mathilde , my dear , how does one tell nowadays whether one is being proposed to or not?"

In this poignant and unexpected crisis Mathilde turned slowly and painfully crimson. How *did* one tell? It was a question which at the moment was anything but clear to her.

"I should always assume it in doubtful cases, sir," said Wayne, very distinctly. He and Mathilde did not even glance at each other.

"It wasn't your proposal that you came to announce to us, though, was it, Papa?" said Adelaide.

"No," answered Mr. Lanley. "The fact is, I've been arrested."

"Again?"

"Yes; most unjustly, most unjustly." His brows contracted, and then relaxed at a happy memory. "It's the long, low build of the car. It looks so powerful that the police won't give you a chance. It was nosing through the park - "

"At about thirty miles an hour," said Farron.

"Well, not a bit over thirty-five. A lovely morning, no one in sight, I may have let her out a little. All of a sudden one of these mounted fellows jumped out from the bushes along the bridle-path. They're a fine-looking lot, Vincent."

Farron asked who the judge was, and, Mr. Lanley named him - named him slightly wrong, and Farron corrected him.

"I'll get you off," he said.

Adelaide looked up at her husband admiringly. This was the aspect of him that she loved best. It seemed to her like magic what Vincent could do. Her father, she thought, took it very calmly. What would have happened to him if she had not brought Farron into the family to rescue and protect? The visiting boy, she noticed, was properly impressed. She saw him give Farron quite a dog-like look as he took his departure. To Mathilde he only bowed. No arrangements had been made for a future meeting. Mathilde tried to convey to him in a prolonged look that if he would wait only five minutes all would be well, that her grandfather never paid long visits; but the door closed behind him. She became immediately overwhelmed by the fear, which had an element of desire in it, too, that her family would fall to discussing him, would question her as to how long she had known him, and why she liked him, and what they talked about, and whether she had been expecting a visit, sitting there in her best dress. Then slowly she took in the fact that they were going to talk about nothing but Mr. Lanley's arrest. She marveled at the obtuseness of older people - to have stood at the red-hot center of youth and love and not even to know it! She drew her shoulders together, feeling very lonely and strong. As they talked, she allowed her eyes to rest first on one speaker and then on the other, as if she were following each word of the discussion. As a matter of fact she was rehearsing with an inner voice the tone of Wayne's voice when he had said that he loved her.

Then suddenly she decided that she would be much happier alone in her own room. She rose, patted her grandfather on the shoulder, and prepared to escape. He, not wishing to be interrupted at the moment, patted her hand in return.

"Hello!" he exclaimed. "Hands are cold, my dear."

She caught Farron's cool, black eyes, and surprised herself by answering:

"Yes; but, then, they always are." This was quite untrue, but every one was perfectly satisfied with it.

As she left the room Mr. Lanley was saying:

"Yes, I don't want to go to Blackwell's Island. Lovely spot, of course. My grandfather used to tell me he remembered it when the Blackwell family still lived there. But I shouldn't care to wear stripes - except for the pleasure of telling Alberta about it. It would give her a year's occupation, her suffering over my disgrace, wouldn't it, Adelaide?"

"She'd scold me," said Adelaide, looking beautifully martyred. Then turning to her husband, she asked. "Will it be very difficult, Vincent, getting papa off?" She wanted it to be difficult, she wanted him to give her material out of which she could form a picture of him as a savior; but he only shook his head and said:

"That young man is in love with Mathilde."

"O Vin! Those children?"

Mr. Lanley pricked up his ears like a terrier.

"In love?" he exclaimed. "And who is he? Not one of the East Sussex Waynes, I hope. Vulgar people. They always were; began life as auctioneers in my father's time. Is he one of those, Adelaide?"

"I have no idea who he is, if any one," said Adelaide. "I never saw or heard of him before this afternoon."

"And may I ask," said her father, "if you intend to let your daughter become engaged to a young man of whom you know nothing whatsoever?"

Adelaide looked extremely languid, one of her methods of showing annoyance.

"Really, Papa," she said, "the fact that he has come once to pay an afternoon visit to Mathilde does not, it seems to me, make an engagement inevitable. My child is not absolutely repellent, you know, and a good many young men come to the house." Then suddenly remembering that her oracle had already spoken on this subject, she asked more humbly, "What was it made you say he was in love, Vin?"

"Just an impression," said Farron.

Mr. Lanley had been thinking it over.

"It was not the custom in my day," he began, and then remembering that this was one of his sister Alberta's favorite openings, he changed the form of his sentence. "I never allowed you to see stray young men -"

His daughter interrupted him.

"But I always saw them, Papa. I used to let them come early in the afternoon before you came in."

In his heart Mr. Lanley doubted that this had been a regular custom, but he knew it would be unwise to argue the point; so he started fresh.

" When a young man is attentive to a girl like Mathilde -"

"But he isn't," said Adelaide. "At least not what I should have called attentive when I was a girl."

"Your experience was not long, my dear. You were married at Mathilde's age."

"You may be sure of one thing, Papa, that I don't desire an early marriage for my daughter."

"Very likely," returned her father, getting up, and buttoning the last button of his coat; "but you may have noticed that we can't always get just what we most desire for our children."

When he had gone, Vincent looked at his wife and smiled, but smiled without approval. She twisted her shoulders.

"Oh, I suppose so," she said; "but I do so hate to be scolded about the way I bring up Mathilde."

"Or about anything else, my dear."

"I don't hate to be scolded by you," she returned. "In fact, I sometimes get a sort of servile enjoyment from it. Besides," she went on, "as a matter of fact, I bring Mathilde up particularly well, quite unlike these wild young women I see everywhere else. She tells me everything, and I have perfectly the power of making her hate any one I disapprove of. But you'll try and find out something about this young man, won't you, Vin?"

"We'll have a full report on him to-morrow. Do you know what his first name is?"

"At the moment I don't recall his last. Oh, yes - Wayne. I'll ask Mathilde when we go up-stairs."

From her own bedroom door she called up.

"Mathilde, what is the name of your young friend?"

There was a little pause before Mathilde answered that she was sorry, but she didn't know.

Alice Duer Miller

Mrs. Farron turned to her husband and made a little gesture to indicate that this ignorance on the girl's part did not bear out his theory; but she saw that he did not admit it, that he clung still to his impression. "And Vincent's impressions -" she said to herself as she went in to dress.

CHAPTER III

Mr. Lanley was ruffled as he left his daughter's drawing-room.

"As if I had wanted her to marry at eighteen," he said to himself; and he took his hat crossly from Pringle and set it hard on his head at the slight angle which he preferred. Then reflecting that Pringle was not in any way involved, he unbent slightly, and said something that sounded like:

"Haryer, Pringle?"

Pringle, despite his stalwart masculine appearance, had in speaking a surprisingly high, squeaky voice.

"I keep my health, thank you, sir," he said. "Anna has been somewhat ailing." Anna was his wife, to whom he usually referred as "Mrs. Pringle"; but he made an exception in speaking to Mr. Lanley, for she had once been the Lanleys' kitchen-maid. "Your car, sir?"

No, Mr. Lanley was walking - walking, indeed, more quickly than usual under the stimulus of annoyance.

Nothing had ever happened that made him suffer as he had suffered through his daughter's divorce. Divorce was one of the modern ideas which he had imagined he

Alice Duer Miller

had accepted. As a lawyer he had expressed himself as willing always to take the lady's side; but in the cases which he actually took he liked to believe that the wife was perfect and the husband inexcusable. He could not comfort himself with any such belief in his daughter's case.

Adelaide's conduct had been, as far as he could see, irreproachable; but, then, so had Severance's. This was what had made the gossip, almost the scandal, of the thing. Even his sister Alberta had whispered to him that if Severance had been unfaithful to Adelaide - But poor Severance had not been unfaithful; he had not even become indifferent. He loved his wife, he said, as much as on the day he married her. He was extremely unhappy. Mr. Lanley grew to dread the visits of his huge, blond son-in-law, who used actually to sob in the library, and ask for explanations of something which Mr. Lanley had never been able to understand.

And how obstinate Adelaide had been! She, who had been such a docile girl, and then for many years so completely under the thumb of her splendid-looking husband, had suddenly become utterly intractable. She would listen to no reason and brook no delay. She had been willing enough to explain; she had explained repeatedly, but the trouble was he could not understand the explanation. She did not love her husband any more, she said. Mr. Lanley pointed out to her that this was no legal grounds for a divorce.

"Yes, but I look down upon him," she went on.

"On poor Joe?" her father had asked innocently, and had then discovered that this was the wrong thing to say. She had burst out, "Poor Joe! Poor Joe!" That was the way every one considered him. Was it her fault if he excited pity and contempt instead of love and respect? Her love, she intimated, had been of a peculiarly eternal sort; Severance himself was to blame for its extinction. Mr. Lanley discovered that in some way she considered the intemperance of Severance's habits to be involved. But this was absurd. It was true that for a year or two Severance had taken to drinking rather more than was wise; but, Mr. Lanley had thought at the time, the poor young man had not needed any artificial stimulant in the days when Adelaide had fully and constantly admired him. He had seen Severance come home several times not exactly drunk, but rather more boyishly boastful and hilarious than usual. Even Mr. Lanley, a naturally temperate man, had not found Joe repellent in the circumstances. Afterward he had been thankful for this weakness: it gave him the only foundation on which he could build a case not for the courts, of course, but for the world. Unfortunately, however, Severance had pulled up before there was any question of divorce.

That was another confusing fact. Adelaide had managed him so beautifully. Her father had not known her wonderful powers until he saw the skill and patience with which she had dealt with Joe Severance's drinking. Joe himself was eager to own that he owed his cure entirely to her. Mr. Lanley had been proud of her; she had turned out, he thought, just what a woman ought to be; and then, on top of it, she had come to him one day and announced that she would never live with Joe again.

"But why not?" he had asked.

"Because I don't love him," she had said.

Then Mr. Lanley knew how little his acceptance of the idea of divorce in general had reconciled him to the idea of the divorce of his own daughter - a Lanley - Mrs. Adelaide Lanley, Mrs. Adelaide Severance. His sense of fitness was shocked, though he pleaded with her first on the ground of duty, and then under the threat of scandal. With her beauty and Severance's popularity, for from his college days he had been extremely popular with men, the divorce excited uncommon interest. Severance's unconcealed grief, a rather large circle of devoted friends in whom he confided, and the fact that Adelaide had to go to Nevada to get her divorce, led most people to believe that she had simply found some one she liked better. Mr. Lanley would have believed it himself, but he couldn't. Farron had not appeared until she had been divorced for several years.

Lanley still cherished an affection for Severance, who had very soon married again, a local belle in the Massachusetts manufacturing town where he now lived. She was said to resemble Adelaide.

No, Mr. Lanley could not see that he had had anything to reproach himself with in regard to his daughter's first marriage. They had been young, of course; all the better. He had known the Severances for years; and Joe was handsome, hard working, had rowed on his crew, and every one spoke well of him. Certainly they had been in love - more in love than he liked to see two people, at least when one of them was his own daughter. He had suggested their waiting a year or two, but no one had backed him up. The Severances had been eager for the marriage, naturally. Mr. Lanley could still see the young couple as they turned from the altar, young, beautiful, and confident.

He had missed his daughter terribly, not only her physical presence in the house, but the exercise of his influence over her, which in old times had been perhaps a trifle autocratic. He had hated being told what Joe thought and said; yet he could hardly object to her docility. That was the way he had brought her up. He did not reckon pliancy in a woman as a weakness; or if he had had any temptation to do so, it had vanished in the period when Joe Severance had taken to drink. In that crisis Adelaide had been anything but weak. Every one had been so grateful to her, - he and Joe and the Severances, - and then immediately afterward the crash came.

Women! Mr. Lanley shook his head, still moving briskly northward with that quick jaunty walk of his. And this second marriage - what about that? They seemed happy. Farron was a fine fellow, but not, it seemed to him, so attractive to a woman as Severance. Could he hold a woman like Adelaide? He wasn't a man to stand any nonsense, though, and Mr. Lanley nodded; then, as it were, withdrew the nod on remembering that poor Joe had not wanted to stand any nonsense either. What in similar circumstances could Farron do? Adelaide always resented his asking how things were going, but how could he help being anxious? How could any one rest content on a hillside who had once been blown up by a volcano?

He might not have been any more content if he had stayed to dinner at his son-in-law's, as he had been asked to do. The Farrons were alone. Mathilde was going to a dinner, with a dance after. She came into the dining-room to say good night and to promise to be home early, not to stay and dance. She was not allowed two parties on successive nights, not because her health was anything but robust, but rather because her mother considered her too young for such vulgar excess.

When she had gone, Farron observed:

"That child has a will of iron."

"Vincent!" said his wife. "She does everything I suggest to her."

"Her will just now is to please you in everything. Wait until she rebels."

"But women don't rebel against the people they love. I don't have to tell you that, do I? I never have to manoeuver the child, never have to coax or charm her to do what I want."

He smiled at her across the table.

"You have great faith in those methods, haven't you?"

"They work, Vin."

He nodded as if no one knew that better than he.

Soon after dinner he went up-stairs to write some letters. She followed him about ten o'clock. She came and leaned one hand on his shoulder and one on his desk.

"Still working?" she said. She had been aware of no desire to see what he was writing, but she was instantly aware that his blotting-paper had fallen across the sheet, that the sheet was not a piece of note-paper, but one of a large pad on which he had been apparently making notes.

Her diamond bracelet had slipped down her wrist and lay upon the blotting-paper; he slowly and carefully pushed it up her slim, round arm until it once more clung in place.

"I've nearly finished," he said; and to her ears there was some under sound of pain or of constraint in his tone.

A little later he strolled, still dressed, into her room. She was already in bed, and he came and sat on the foot of the bed, with one foot tucked under him and his arms folded.

Her mind during the interval had been exclusively occupied with the position of that piece of blotting-paper. Could it be there was some other woman whose ghost-like presence she was just beginning to feel haunting their relation? The impersonality of Vincent's manner was an armor against such attacks, but this armor, as Adelaide knew, was more apparent than real. If one could get beyond that, one was at the very heart of the man. If some fortuitous circumstance had brought a sudden accidental intimacy between him and another woman - What woman loving strength and power could resist the sight of Vincent in action, Vincent as she saw him?

Yet with a good capacity for believing the worst of her fellow-creatures, Adelaide did not really believe in the other woman. That, she knew, would bring a change in the fundamentals of her relationship with her husband. This was only a barrier that left the relation

Alice Duer Miller

itself untouched.

Before very long she began to think the situation was all in her own imagination. He was so amused, so eager to talk. Silent as he was apt to be with the rest of the world, with her he sometimes showed a love of gossip that enchanted her. And now it seemed to her that he was leading her on from subject to subject through a childish dislike to going to bed. They were actually giggling over Mr. Lanley's adventure when a motor-brake squeaked in the silence of the night, a motor-door slammed. For the first time Adelaide remembered her daughter. It was after twelve o'clock. A knock came at her door. She wrapped her swan's-down garment about her and went to the door.

"O Mama, have you been worried?" the girl asked. She was standing in the narrow corridor, with her arms full of shining favors; there could be no question whatever that she had stayed for the dance. "Are you angry? Have I been keeping you awake?"

"I thought you would have been home an hour ago."

"I know. I want to tell you about it. Mama, how lovely you look in that blue thing! Won't you come up-stairs with me while I undress?"

Adelaide shook her head.

"Not to-night," she answered.

"You are angry with me," the girl went on. "But if you will come, I will explain. I have something to tell you, Mama."

Mrs. Farron's heart stood still. The phrase could mean only one thing. She went up-stairs with her daughter, sent the maid away, and herself began to undo the soft, pink silk.

"It needs an extra hook," she murmured. "I told her it did."

Mathilde craned her neck over her shoulder, as if she had ever been able to see the middle of her back.

"But it doesn't show, does it?" she asked.

"It perfectly well might."

Mathilde stepped out of her dress, and flung it over a chair. In her short petticoat, with her ankles showing and her arms bare, she looked like a very young girl, and when she put up her hands and took the pins out of her hair, so that it fell over her shoulders, she might have been a child.

The silence began to grow awkward. Mathilde put on her dressing-gown; it was perfectly straight, and made her look like a little white column. A glass of milk and some biscuits were waiting for her. She pushed a chair near her fire for her mother, and herself remained standing, with her glass of milk in her hand.

"Mama," she said suddenly, "I suppose I'm what you'd call engaged."

"O Mathilde! not to that boy who was here to-day?"

"Why not to him?"

"I know nothing about him."

"I don't know very much myself. Yes, it's Pete Wayne. Pierson his name is, but every one calls him Pete. How strange it was that I did not even know his first name when you asked me!"

A single ray pierced Mrs. Farron's depression: Vincent had known, Vincent's infallibility was confirmed. She did not know what to say. She sat looking sadly, obliquely at the floor like a person who has been aggrieved. She was wondering whether she should be to her daughter a comrade or a ruler, a confederate or a policeman. Of course in all probability the thing would be better stopped. But could this be accomplished by immediate action, or could she invite confidences and yet commit herself to nothing?

She raised her eyes.

"I do not approve of youthful marriages," she said.

"O Mama! And you were only eighteen yourself."

"That is why."

Mathilde was frightened not only by the intense bitterness of her mother's tone, but also by the obvious fact that she was face to face with the explanation of the separation of her parents. She had been only nine years old at the time. She had loved her father, had found him a better playfellow than her mother, had wept bitterly at parting with him, and had missed him. And then gradually her mother, who had before seemed like a beautiful, but remote, princess, had begun to make of her an intimate and grown-up friend, to consult her and read with her and arrange happinesses in her life, to win, to, if the truth must be told, reconquer her. Perhaps even Adelaide would not have succeeded so easily in effacing Severance's image had not he himself so quickly remarried. Mathilde went several times to stay with the new household after Adelaide in secret, tearful conference with her father had been forced to consent.

To Mathilde these visits had been an unacknowledged torture. She never knew quite what to mention and what to leave untouched. There was always a constraint between the three of them. Her father, when alone with her, would question her, with strange, eager pauses, as to how her mother looked. Her mother's successor, whom she could not really like, would question her more searchingly, more embarrassingly, with an ill-concealed note of jealousy in every word. Even at twelve years Mathilde was shocked by the strain of hatred in her father's new wife, who seemed to reproach her for fashion and fineness and fastidiousness, qualities of which the girl was utterly unaware. She could have loved her little half-brother when he appeared upon the scene, but Mrs. Severance did not encourage the bond, and gradually Mathilde's visits to her father ceased.

As a child she had been curious about the reasons for the parting, but as she grew older it had seemed mere loyalty to accept the fact without asking why; she had perhaps not wanted to know why. But now, she saw, she was to hear.

"Mathilde, do you still love your father?"

"I think I do, Mama. I feel very sorry for him."

"Why?"

"I don't know why. I dare say he is happy."

"I dare say he is, poor Joe." Adelaide paused. "Well, my dear, that was the reason of our parting. One can pity a son or a brother, but not a husband. Weakness kills love. A woman cannot be the leader, the guide, and keep any romance. O Mathilde, I never want you to feel the humiliation of finding yourself stronger than the man you love. That is why I left your father, and my justification is his present happiness. This inferior little person he has married, she does as well. Any one would have done as well."

Mathilde was puzzled by her mother's evident conviction that the explanation was complete. She asked after a moment:

"But what was it that made you think at first that you did love him, Mama?"

"Just what makes you think you love this boy - youth, flattery, desire to love. He was magnificently hand-some, your father. I saw him admired by other men, apparently a master; I was too young to judge, my dear. You shan't be allowed to make that mistake; you shall have time to consider."

Mathilde smiled.

"I don't want time," she said.

"I did not know I did."

"I don't think I feel about love as you do," said the

girl, slowly.

"Every woman does."

Mathilde shook her head.

"It's just Pete as he is that I love. I don't care which of us leads."

"But you will."

The girl had not yet reached a point where she could describe the very essence of her passion; she had to let this go. After a moment she said:

"I see now why you chose Mr. Farron."

"You mean you have never seen before?"

"Not so clearly."

Mrs. Farron bit her lips. To have missed understanding this seemed a sufficient proof of immaturity. She rose.

"Well, my darling," she said in a tone of extreme reasonableness, "we shall decide nothing to-night. I know nothing against Mr. Wayne. He may be just the right person. We must see more of him. Do you know anything about his family?"

Mathilde shook her head. "He lives alone with his mother. His father is dead. She's very good and interested in drunkards."

"In *drunkards*?" Mrs. Farron just shut her eyes a second.

"She has a mission that reforms them."

"Is that his profession, too?"

"Oh, no. He's in Wall Street - quite a good firm. O Mama, don't sigh like that! We know we can't be married at once. We are reasonable. You think not, because this has all happened so suddenly; but great things do happen suddenly. We love each other. That's all I wanted to tell you."

"Love!" Adelaide looked at the little person before her, tried to recall the fading image of the young man, and then thought of the dominating figure in her own life. "My dear, you have no idea what love is."

She took no notice of the queer, steady look the girl gave her in return. She went down-stairs. She had been gone more than an hour, and she knew that Vincent would have been long since asleep. He had, and prided himself on having, a great capacity for sleep. She tiptoed past his door, stole into her own room, and then, glancing in the direction of his, was startled to see that a light was burning. She went in; he was reading, and once again, as his eyes turned toward her, she thought she saw the same tragic appeal that she had felt that afternoon in his kiss. Trembling, she threw herself down beside him, clasping him to her.

"O Vincent! oh, my dear!" she whispered, and began to cry. He did not ask her why she was crying; she wished that he would; his silence admitted that he knew of some adequate reason.

"I feel that there is something wrong," she sobbed, "something terribly wrong."

"Nothing could go wrong between you and me, my darling," he answered. His tone comforted, his touch was a comfort. Perhaps she was a coward, she said to herself, but she questioned him no further.

CHAPTER IV

Wayne was not so prompt as Mathilde in making the announcement of their engagement. He and his mother breakfasted together rather hastily, for she was going to court that morning to testify in favor of one of her backsliding inebriates, and Wayne had not found the moment to introduce his own affairs.

That afternoon he came home earlier than usual; it was not five o'clock. He passed Dr. Parret's flat on the first floor - Dr. Lily MacComb Parret. She was a great friend of his, and he felt a decided temptation to go in and tell her the news first; but reflecting that no one ought to hear it before his mother, he went on up-stairs. He lived on the fifth floor.

He opened the door of the flat and went into the sitting-room. It was empty. He lighted the gas, which flared up, squeaking like a bagpipe. The room was square and crowded. Shelves ran all the way round it, tightly filled with books. In the center was a large writing-table, littered with papers, and on each side of the fireplace stood two worn, but comfortable, arm-chairs, each with a reading-lamp at its side. There was nothing beautiful in the furniture, and yet the room had its own charm. The house was a corner house and had once been a single dwelling. The shape of the room, its woodwork, its doors, its flat, white marble mantelpiece, belonged to an era of simple taste and good workmanship; but the greatest charm of the room was the view from the windows, of which it had four, two that looked east and two south, and gave a glimpse of the East River and its bridges.

Wayne was not sorry his mother was out. He had begun to dread the announcement he had to make. At first he had thought only of her keen interest in his affairs, but later he had come to consider what this particular piece of news would mean to her. Say what you will, he thought, to tell your mother of your engagement is a little like casting off an old love.

Ever since he could remember, he and his mother had lived in the happiest comradeship. His father, a promising young doctor, had died within a few years of his marriage. Pete had been brought up by his mother, but he had very little remembrance of any process of molding. It seemed to him as if they had lived in a sort of partnership since he had been able to walk and talk. It had been as natural for him to spend his hours after school in stamping and sealing her large correspondence as it had been for her to pinch and arrange for years so as to send him to the university from which his father had been graduated. She would have been glad, he knew, if he had decided to follow his father in the study of medicine, but he recoiled from so long a period of dependence; he liked to think that he brought to his financial reports something of a scientific inheritance.

She had, he thought, every virtue that a mother could have, and she combined them with a gaiety of spirit that made her take her virtues as if they were the most delightful amusements. It was of this gaiety that he had

Alice Duer Miller

first thought until Mathilde had pointed out to him that there was tragedy in the situation. "What will your mother do without you?" the girl kept saying. There was indeed nothing in his mother's life that could fill the vacancy he would leave. She had few intimate relationships. For all her devotion to her drunkards, he was the only personal happiness in her life.

He went into the kitchen in search of her. This was evidently one of their servant's uncounted hours. While he was making himself some tea he heard his mother's key in the door. He called to her, and she appeared.

"Why my hat, Mother dear?" he asked gently as he kissed her.

Mrs. Wayne smiled absently, and put up her hand to the soft felt hat she was wearing.

"I just went out to post some letters," she said, as if this were a complete explanation; then she removed a mackintosh that she happened to have on, though the day was fine. She was then seen to be wearing a dark skirt and a neat plain shirt that was open at the throat. Though no longer young, she somehow suggested a boy - a boy rather overtrained; she was far more boyish than Wayne. She had a certain queer beauty, too; not beauty of Adelaide's type, of structure and coloring and elegance, but beauty of expression. Life itself had written some fine lines of humor and resolve upon her face, and her blue-gray eyes seemed actually to flare with hope and intention. Her hair was of that light-brown shade in which plentiful gray made little change of shade; it was wound in a knot at the back of her head and gave her trouble. She was always pushing it up and repinning it into place, as if it were too heavy for her small head.

"I wonder if there's anything to eat in the house," her son said.

"I wonder." They moved together toward the ice-box.

"Mother," said Pete, "that piece of pie has been in the ice-box at least three days. Let's throw it away."

She took the saucer thoughtfully.

"I like it so much," she said.

"Then why don't you eat it?"

"It's not good for me." She let Wayne take the saucer. "What do you know?" she asked.

She had adopted slang as she adopted most labor-saving devices.

"Well, I do know something new," said Wayne. He sat down on the kitchen table and poured out his tea. "New as the garden of Eden. I'm in love."

"O Pete!" his mother cried, and the purest, most conventional maternal agony was in the tone. For an instant, crushed and terrified, she looked at him; and then something gay and impish appeared in her eyes, and she asked with a grin:

"Is it some one perfectly awful?"

"I'm afraid you'll think so. She's a sheltered, young, luxurious child, with birth, breeding, and money, everything you hate most."

"O Pete!" she said again, but this time with a sort of sad resignation. Then shaking her head as if to say that she wasn't, after all, as narrow as he thought, she hitched her chair nearer the table and said eagerly, "Well, tell me all about it."

Wayne looked down at his mother as she sat opposite him, with her elbows on the table, as keen as a child and as lively as a cricket. He asked himself if he had not drifted into a needlessly sentimental state of mind about her. He even asked himself, as he had done once or twice before in his life, whether her love for him implied the slightest dependence upon his society. Wasn't it perfectly possible that his going would free her life, would make it easier instead of harder? Every man, he knew, felt the element of freedom beneath the despair of breaking even the tenderest of ties. Some women, he supposed, might feel the same way about their love-affairs. But could they feel the same about their maternal relations? Could it be that his mother, that pure, heroic, self-sacrificing soul, was now thinking more about her liberty than her loss? Had not their relation always been peculiarly free? he found himself thinking reproachfully. Once, he remembered, when he had been working unusually hard he had welcomed her absence at one of her conferences on inebriety. Never before had he imagined that she could feel anything but regret at his absences. "Everybody is just alike," he found himself rather bitterly thinking.

"What do you want to know about it?" he said aloud.

"Why, everything," she returned.

"I met her," he said, "two evenings ago at a dance. I never expected to fall in love at a dance."

"Isn't it funny? No one ever really expects to fall in love at all, and everybody does."

He glanced at her. He had been prepared to explain to her about love; and now it occurred to him for the first time that she knew all about it. He decided to ask her the great question which had been occupying his mind as a lover of a scientific habit of thought.

"Mother," he said, "how much dependence is to be placed on love - one's own, I mean?"

"Goodness, Pete! What a question to ask!"

"Well, you might take a chance and tell me what you think. I have no doubts. My whole nature goes out to this girl; but I can't help knowing that if we go on feeling like this till we die, we shall be the exception. Love's a miracle. How much can one trust to it?"

The moment he had spoken he knew that he was asking a great deal. It was torture to his mother to express an opinion on an abstract question. She did not lack decision of conduct. She could resolve in an instant to send a drunkard to an institution or take a trip round the world; but on a matter of philosophy of life it was as difficult to get her to commit herself as if she had been upon the witness-stand. Yet it was just in this realm that he particularly valued her opinion.

"Oh," she said at last, "I don't believe that it's possible to play safe in love. It's a risk, but it's one of those risks you haven't much choice about taking. Life and death are like that, too. I don't think it pays to be always thinking about avoiding risks. Nothing, you know," she added, as if she were letting him in to rather a horrid little secret, "is really safe." And evidently glad to change the subject, she went on, "What will her family say?"

"I can't think they will be pleased."

"I suppose not. Who are they?"

Wayne explained the family connections, but woke no associations in his mother's mind until he mentioned the name of Farron. Then he was astonished at the violence of her interest. She sprang to her feet; her eyes lighted up.

"Why," she cried, "that's the man, that's the company, that Marty Burke works for! O Pete, don't you think you could get Mr. Farron to use his influence over Marty about Anita?"

"Dear mother, do you think you can get him to use his influence over Mrs. Farron for me?"

Marty Burke was the leader of the district and was reckoned a bad man. He and Mrs. Wayne had been waging a bitter war for some time over a young inebriate who had seduced a girl of the neighborhood. Mrs. Wayne was sternly trying to prosecute the inebriate; Burke was determined to protect him, first, by smirching the girl's name, and, next, by getting the girl's family to consent to a marriage, a solution that Mrs. Wayne considered most undesirable in view of the character of the prospective husband.

Pete felt her interest sweep away from his affairs, and it had not returned when the telephone rang. He came back from answering it to tell his mother that Mr. Lanley, the grandfather of his love, was asking if she would see him for a few minutes that afternoon or evening. A visit was arranged for nine o'clock.

"What's he like?" asked Mrs. Wayne, wrinkling her nose and looking very impish.

"He seemed like a nice old boy; hasn't had a new idea, I should say, since 1880. And, Mother dear, you're going to dress, aren't you?"

She resented the implication.

"I shall be wonderful," she answered with emphasis. "And while he's here, I think you might go down and tell this news to Lily, yourself. Oh, I don't say she's in love with you - "

"Lily," said Pete, "is leading far too exciting a life to be in love with any one."

Punctually at nine, Mr. Lanley rang the bell of the flat. He had paused a few minutes before doing so, not wishing to weaken the effect of his mission by arriving out of breath. Adelaide had come to see him just before lunch. She pretended to minimize the importance of her news, but he knew she did so to evade reproach for the culpable irresponsibility of her attitude toward the young man's first visit.

"And do you know anything more about him than you did yesterday?" he asked.

She did. It appeared that Vincent had telephoned her from down town just before she came out.

"Tiresome young man," she said, twisting her shoulders. "It seems there's nothing against him. His father was a doctor, his mother comes of decent people and is a respected reformer, the young man works for an ambitious new firm of brokers, who speak highly of him and give him a salary of $5000 a year."

"The whole thing must be put a stop to," said Mr. Lanley.

"Of course, of course," said his daughter. "But how? I can't forbid him the house because he's just an average young man."

"I don't see why not, or at least on the ground that he's not the husband you would choose for her."

"I think the best way will be to let him come to the house," - she spoke with a sort of imperishable sweetness, - "but to turn Mathilde gradually against him."

"But how can you turn her against him?"

Adelaide looked very wistful.

"You don't trust me," she moaned.

"I only ask you how it can be done."

"Oh, there are ways. I made her perfectly hate one of them because he always said, 'if you know what I mean.' 'It's a very fine day, Mrs. Farron, if you know what I mean.' This young man must have some horrid trick like that, only I haven't studied him yet. Give me time."

"It's risky."

Adelaide shook her head.

"Not really," she said. "These young fancies go as quickly as they come. Do you remember the time you took me to West Point? I had a passion for the adjutant. I forgot him in a week."

"You were only fifteen."

"Mathilde is immature for her age."

It was agreed between them, however, that Mr. Lanley, without authority, should go and look the situation over. He had been trying to get the Waynes' telephone since one o'clock. He had been told at intervals of fifteen minutes by a resolutely cheerful central that their number did not answer. Mr. Lanley hated people who did not answer their telephone. Nor was he agreeably impressed by the four flights of stairs, or by the appearance of the servant who answered his ring.

"Won't do, won't do," he kept repeating in his own mind.

He was shown into the sitting-room. It was in shadow, for only a shaded reading-lamp was lighted, and his first impression was of four windows; they appeared like four square panels of dark blue, patterned with stars. Then a figure rose to meet him - a figure in blue draperies , with heavy braids wound around the head,

Alice Duer Miller

and a low, resonant voice said, "I am Mrs. Wayne."

As soon as he could he walked to the windows and looked out to the river and the long, lighted curves of the bridges, and beyond to Long Island, to just the ground where the Battle of Long Island had been fought - a battle in which an ancestor of his had particularly distinguished himself. He said something polite about the view.

"Let us sit here where we can look out," she said, and sank down on a low sofa drawn under the windows. As she did so she came within the circle of light from the lamp. She sat with her head leaned back against the window-frame, and he saw the fine line of her jaw, the hollows in her cheek, the delicate modeling about her brows, not obscured by much eyebrow, and her long, stretched throat. She was not quite maternal enough to look like a Madonna, but she did look like a saint, he thought.

He knelt with one knee on the couch and peered out.

"Dear me," he said, "I fancy I used to skate as a boy on a pond just about where that factory is now."

He found she knew very little about the history of New York. She had been brought up abroad, she said; her father had been a consul in France. It was a subject which he liked to expound. He loved his native city, which he with his own eyes had seen once as hardly more than a village. He and his ancestors - and Mr. Lanley's sense of identification with his ancestors was almost Chinese - had watched and had a little shaped the growth.

"I suppose you had Dutch ancestry, then," she said, trying to take an interest.

"Dutch." Mr. Lanley shut his eyes, resolving, since he had no idea what her own descent might be, that he would not explain to her the superior attitude of the English settlers of the eighteenth century toward their Dutch predecessors. However, perhaps he did not entirely conceal his feeling, for he said: "No, I have no Dutch blood - not a drop. Very good people in their way, industrious - peasants." He hurried on to the great fire of 1835. "Swept between Wall Street and Coenties Slip," he said, with a splendid gesture, and then discovered that she had, never heard of "Quenches Slip," or worse, she had pronounced it as it was spelled. He gently set her right there. His father had often told him that he had seen with his own eyes a note of hand which had been blown, during the course of the conflagration, as far as Flatbush. And the second fire of 1845. His father had been a man then, married, a prominent citizen, old enough, as Mr. Lanley said, with a faint smile, to have lost heavily. He could himself remember the New York of the Civil War, the bitter family quarrels, the forced resignations from clubs, the duels, the draft riots.

But, oddly enough, when it came to contemporary New York, it was Mrs. Wayne who turned out to be most at home. Had he ever walked across the Blackwell's Island Bridge? (This was in the days before it bore the elevated trains.) No, he had driven. Ah, she said, that was wholly different. Above, where one walked, there was nothing to shut out the view of the river. Just to show that he was not a feeble old antiquarian, he suggested their taking a walk there at once. She held out her trailing garments and thin, blue

Alice Duer Miller

slippers. And then she went on:

"There's another beautiful place I don't believe you know, for all you're such an old New-Yorker - a pier at the foot of East Eighty-something Street, where you can almost touch great seagoing vessels as they pass."

"Well, there at least we can go," said Mr. Lanley, and he stood up. "I have a car here, but it's open. Is it too cold? Have you a fur coat? I'll send back to the house for an extra one." He paused, brisk as he was; the thought of those four flights a second time dismayed him.

The servant had gone out, and Pete was still absent, presumably breaking the news of his engagement to Dr. Parret.

Mrs. Wayne had an idea. She went to a window on the south side of the room, opened it, and looked out. If he had good lungs, she told him, he could make his man hear.

Mr. Lanley did not visibly recoil. He leaned out and shouted. The chauffeur looked up, made a motion to jump out, fearing that his employer was being murdered in these unfamiliar surroundings; then he caught the order to go home for an extra coat.

Lanley drew his shoulder back into the room and shut the window; as he did so he saw a trace of something impish in the smile of his hostess.

"Why do you smile?" he asked quickly.

She did not make the mistake of trying to arrest her

smile; she let it broaden.

"I don't suppose you have ever done such a thing before."

"Now, that does annoy me."

"Calling down five stories?"

"No; your thinking I minded."

"Well, I did think so."

"You were mistaken, utterly mistaken."

"I'm glad. If you mind doing such things, you give so much time to arranging not to do them."

Mr. Lanley was silent. He was deciding that he should rearrange some of the details of his life. Not that he contemplated giving all his orders from the fifth story, but he saw he had always devoted too much attention to preventing unimportant catastrophes.

Under her direction he was presently driving north; then he turned sharply east down a little hill, and came out on a low, flat pier. He put out the motor's lights. They were only a few feet above the water, which was as black as liquid jet, with flat silver and gold patches on it from white and yellow lights. Opposite to them the lighthouse at the north end of Blackwell's Island glowed like a hot coal. Then a great steamer obscured it.

"Isn't this nice?" Mrs. Wayne asked, and he saw that she wanted her discovery praised. He never lost the impression that she enjoyed being praised.

Such a spot, within sight of half a dozen historic sites, was a temptation to Mr. Lanley, and he would have unresistingly yielded to it if Mrs. Wayne had not said:

"But we haven't said a word yet about our children."

"True," answered Mr. Lanley. His heart sank. It is not easy, he thought, to explain to a person for whom you have just conceived a liking that her son had aspired above his station. He tapped his long, middle finger on the steering-wheel, just as at directors' meetings he tapped the table before he spoke, and began, "In a society somewhat artificially formed as ours is, Mrs. Wayne, it has always been my experience that - " Do what he would, it kept turning into a speech, and the essence of the speech was that while democracy did very well for men, a strictly aristocratic system was the only thing possible for girls - one's own girls, of course. In the dim light he could see that she had pushed all her hair back from her brows. She was trying to follow him exactly, so exactly that she confused him a little. He became more general. "In many ways," he concluded, "the advantages of character and experience are with the lower classes." He had not meant to use the word, but when it slipped out, he did not regret it.

"In all ways," she answered.

He was not sure he had heard.

"All the advantages?" he said.

"All the advantages of character."

He had to ask her to explain. One reason, perhaps, why Mrs. Wayne habitually avoided a direct question was that, when once started, her candor had no bounds. Now she began to speak. She spoke more eagerly and more fluently than he, and it took him several minutes to see that quite unconsciously she was making him a strange, distorted complement to his speech, that in her mouth such words as "the leisure classes, your sheltered girls," were terms of the deepest reproach. He must understand, she said, that as she did not know Miss Severance, there was nothing personal, nothing at all personal, in her feeling, - she was as careful not to hurt his feelings as he had tried to be not to hurt hers, - but she did own to a prejudice - at least Pete told her it was a prejudice -

Against what, in Heaven's name, Lanley at first wondered; and then it came to him.

"Oh, you have a prejudice against divorce?" he said.

Mrs. Wayne looked at him reproachfully.

"Oh, no," she answered. "How could you think that? But what has divorce to do with it? Your grand-daughter hasn't been divorced."

A sound of disgust at the mere suggestion escaped him, and he said coldly:

"My daughter divorced her first husband."

"Oh, I did not know."

"Against what, then, is this unconquerable prejudice of yours?"

"Against the daughters of the leisure class."

He was still quite at sea.

"You dislike them?"

"I fear them."

If she had said that she considered roses a menace, he could not have been more puzzled. He repeated her words aloud, as if he hoped that they might have some meaning for him if he heard his own lips pronouncing them:

"You fear them."

"Yes," she went on, now interested only in expressing her belief, "I fear their ignorance and idleness and irresponsibility and self-indulgence, and, all the more because it is so delicate and attractive and unconscious; and their belief that the world owes them luxury and happiness without their lifting a finger. I fear their cowardice and lack of character - "

"Cowardice!" he cried, catching at the first word he could. "My dear Mrs. Wayne, the aristocrats in the French Revolution, the British officer - "

"Oh, yes, they know how to die," she answered; "but do they know how to live when the horrible, sordid little strain of every-day life begins to make demands upon them, their futile education, the moral feebleness that comes with perfect safety! I know something can be made of such girls, but I don't want my son sacrificed in the process."

There was a long, dark silence; then Mr. Lanley said with a particularly careful and exact enunciation:

"I think, my dear madam, that you cannot have known very many of the young women you are describing. It may be that there are some like that - daughters of our mushroom finance; but I can assure you that the children of ladies and gentlemen are not at all as you seem to imagine."

It was characteristic of Mrs. Wayne that, still absorbed by her own convictions, she did not notice the insult of hearing ladies and gentlemen described to her as if they were beings wholly alien to her experience; but the tone of his speech startled her, and she woke, like a person coming out of a trance, to all the harm she had done.

"I may be old-fashioned - " he began and then threw the phrase from him; it was thus that Alberta, his sister, began her most offensive pronouncements. "It has always appeared to me that we shelter our more favored women as we shelter our planted trees, so that they may attain a stronger maturity."

"But do they, are they - are sheltered women the strongest in a crisis?"

Fiend in human shape, he thought, she was making him question his bringing up of Adelaide. He would not bear that. His foot stole out to the self-starter.

For the few minutes that remained of the interview she tried to undo her work, but the injury was too deep. His life was too near its end for criticism to be anything but destructive; having no time to collect new treasure, he simply could not listen to her suggestion that those he most valued were imitation. He hated her for holding such opinion. Her soft tones, her eager concessions, her flattering sentences, could now make no impression upon a man whom half an hour before they would have completely won.

He bade her a cold good night, hardly more than bent his head, the chauffeur took the heavy coat from her, and the car had wheeled away before she was well inside her own doorway.

Pete's brown head was visible over the banisters.

"Hello, Mother!" he said. "Did the old boy kidnap you?"

Mrs. Wayne came up slowly, stumbling over her long, blue draperies in her weariness and depression.

"Oh, Pete, my darling," she said, "I think I've spoiled everything."

His heart stood still. He knew better than most people that his mother could either make or mar.

"They won't hear of it?"

She nodded distractedly.

"I do make such a mess of things sometimes!"

He put his arm about her.

"So you do, Mother," he said; "but then think how magnificently you sometimes pull them out again."

CHAPTER V

Mr. Lanley had not reported the result of his interview immediately. He told himself that it was too late; but it was only a quarter before eleven when he was back safe in his own library, feeling somehow not so safe as usual. He felt attacked, insulted; and yet he also felt vivified and encouraged. He felt as he might have felt if some one, unbidden, had cut a vista on the Lanley estates, first outraged in his sense of property, but afterward delighted with the widened view and the fresher breeze. It was awkward, though, that he didn't want Adelaide to go into details as to his visit; he did not think that the expedition to the pier could be given the judicial, grandfatherly tone that he wanted to give. So he did not communicate at all with his daughter that night.

The next morning about nine, however, when she was sitting up in bed, with her tray on her knees, and on her feet a white satin coverlet sown as thickly with bright little flowers as the Milky Way with stars, her last words to Vincent, who was standing by the fire, with his newspaper folded in his hands, ready to go down-town, were interrupted, as they nearly always were, by the burr of the telephone.

She took it up from the table by her bed, and as she did so she fixed her eyes on her husband and looked steadily at him all the time that central was making the connection; she was trying to answer that unsolved problem as to whether or not a mist hung between them. Then she got her connection.

"Yes, Papa; it is Adelaide." "Yes?" "Did she appear like a lady?" "A lady?" "You don't know what I mean by that? Why, Papa!" "Well, did she appear respectable?" "How cross you are to me!" "I'm glad to hear it. You did not sound cheerful."

She hung up the receiver and turned to Vincent, making eyes of surprise.

"Really, papa is too strange. Why should he be cross to me because he has had an unsatisfactory interview with the Wayne boy's mother? I never wanted him to go, anyhow, Vin. I wanted to send *you*."

"It would probably be better for you to go yourself."

He left the room as if he had said nothing remarkable. But it was remarkable, in Adelaide's experience, that he should avoid any responsibility, and even more so that he should shift it to her shoulders. For an instant she faced the possibility, the most terrible of any that had occurred to her, that the balance was changing between them; that she, so willing to be led, was to be forced to guide. She had seen it happen so often between married couples - the weight of character begin on one side of the scale, and then slowly the beam would shift. Once it had happened to her. Was it to happen again? No, she told herself; never with Farron. He would command or die, lead her or leave her.

Mathilde knocked at her door, as she did every morning as soon as her stepfather had gone down town. She had had an earlier account of Mr. Lanley's interview. It had read:

"DEAREST GIRL:

"The great discussion did not go very well, apparently. The opinion prevails at the moment that no engagement can be allowed to exist between us. I feel as if they were all meeting to discuss whether or not the sun is to rise to-morrow morning. You and I, my love, have special information that it will."

After this it needed no courage to go down and hear her mother's account of the interview. Adelaide was still in bed, but one long, pointed fingertip, pressed continuously upon the dangling bell, a summons that had long since lost its poignancy for the temperamental Lucie, indicated that she was about to get up.

"My dear," she said in answer to Mathilde's question, "your grandfather's principal interest seems to be to tell me nothing at all, and he has been wonderfully successful. I can get nothing from him, so I'm going myself."

The girl's heart sank at hearing this. Her mother saw things clearly and definitely, and had a talent for expressing her impressions in unforgetable words. Mathilde could still remember with a pang certain books, poems, pictures, and even people whose charms her mother had destroyed in one poisonous phrase. Adelaide was too careful of her personal dignity to indulge in mimicry, but she had a way of catching and repeating the exact phrasing of some foolish sentence

Alice Duer Miller

that was almost better - or worse - than mimicry. Mathilde remembered a governess, a kind and patient person of whom Adelaide had greatly wearied, who had a habit of beginning many observations, "It may strike you as strange, but I am the sort of person who - " Mathilde was present at luncheon one day when Adelaide was repeating one of these sentences. "It may strike you as strange, but I like to feel myself in good health." Mathilde resented the laughter that followed, and sprang to her governess's defense, yet sickeningly soon she came to see the innocent egotism that directed the choice of the phrase.

She felt as if she could not bear this process to be turned against Pete's mother, not because it would alter the respectful love she was prepared to offer this unknown figure, but because it might very slightly alter her attitude toward her own mother. That was one of the characteristics of this great emotion: all her old beliefs had to be revised to accord with new discoveries.

This was what lay behind the shrinking of her soul as she watched her mother dress for the visit to Mrs. Wayne. For the first time in her life Mathilde wished that her mother was not so elaborate. Hitherto she had always gloried in Adelaide's elegance as a part of her beauty; but now, as she watched the ritual of ribbons and laces and perfumes and jewels, she felt vaguely that there was in it all a covert insult to Pete's mother, who, she knew, would not be a bit like that.

"How young you are, Mama!" she exclaimed as, the whole long process complete, Adelaide stood holding out her hand for her gloves, like a little girl ready for a party.

Her mother smiled.

"It's well I am," she said, "if you go on trying to get yourself involved with young men who live up four flights of stairs. I have always avoided even dress-makers who lived above the second story," she added wistfully.

The wistful tone was repeated when her car stopped at the Wayne door and she stepped out.

"Are you sure this is the number, Andrews?" she asked. She and the chauffeur looked slowly up at the house and up and down the street. They were at one in their feeling about it. Then Adelaide gave a very gentle little sigh and started the ascent.

The flat did not look as well by day. Though the eastern sun poured in cheerfully, it revealed worn places on the backs of the arm-chairs and one fearful calamity with an ink-bottle that Pete had once had on the rug. Even Mrs. Wayne, who sprang up from behind her writing-table, had not the saint-like mystery that her blue draperies had given her the evening before.

Though slim, and in excellent condition for thirty-nine, Adelaide could not conceal that four flights were an exertion. Her fine nostrils were dilated and her breath not perfectly under control as she said:

"How delightful this is!" a statement that was no more untrue than to say good-morning on a rainy day.

Most women in Mrs. Wayne's situation would at the moment have been acutely aware of the ink-spot. That was one of Adelaide's assets, on which she perhaps unconsciously counted, that her mere appearance made nine people out of ten aware of their own physical imperfections. But Mrs. Wayne was aware of nothing but Adelaide's great beauty as she sank into one of the armchairs with hardly a hint of exhaustion.

"Your son is a very charming person, Mrs. Wayne," she said.

Mrs. Wayne was standing by the mantelpiece, looking boyish and friendly; but now she suddenly grew grave, as if something serious had been said.

"Pete has something more unusual than charm," she said.

"But what could be more unusual?" cried Adelaide, who wanted to add, "The only question is, does your wretched son possess it?" But she didn't; she asked instead, with a tone of disarming sweetness, "Shall we be perfectly candid with each other?"

A quick gleam came into Mrs. Wayne's eyes. "Not much," she seemed to say. She had learned to distrust nothing so much as her own candor, and her interview with Mr. Lanley had put her specially on her guard.

"I hope you will be candid, Mrs. Farron," she said aloud, and for her this was the depth of dissimulation.

"Well, then," said Adelaide, "you and I are in about the same position, aren't we? We are both willing that our children should marry, and we have no objection to offer to their choice except our own ignorance. We both want time to judge. But how can we get time, Mrs. Wayne? If we do not take definite action *against* an engagement, we are giving our consent to it. I want a little reasonable delay, but we can get delay only by refusing to hear of an engagement. Do you see what I mean? Will you help me by pretending to be a very stern parent, just so that these young people may have a few months to think it over without being too definitely committed?"

Mrs. Wayne shrank back. She liked neither diplomacy nor coercion.

"But I have really no control over Pete," she said.

"Surely, if he isn't in a position to support a wife - "

"He is, if she would live as he does."

Such an idea had never crossed Mrs. Farron's mind. She looked round her wonderingly, and said without a trace of wilful insolence in her tone:

"Live here, you mean?"

"Yes, or somewhere like it."

Mrs. Farron looked down, and smoothed the delicate dark fur of her muff. She hardly knew how to begin at the very beginning like this. She did not want to hurt any one's feelings. How could she tell this childlike, optimistic creature that to put Mathilde to living in surroundings like these would be like exposing a naked baby on a mountaintop? It wasn't love of luxury, at least not if luxury meant physical self-indulgence. She could imagine suffering privations very happily in a Venetian palace or on a tropical island. It was an esthetic, not a moral, problem; it was a question of that

Alice Duer Miller

profound and essential thing in the life of any woman who was a woman - her charm. She wished to tell Mrs. Wayne that her son wouldn't really like it, that he would hate to see Mathilde going out in overshoes; that the background that she, Adelaide, had so expertly provided for her child was part of the very attraction that made him want to take her out of it. There was no use in saying that most poor mortals were forced to get on without this magic atmosphere. They had never been goddesses; they did not know what they were going without. But her child, who had been, as it were, born a fairy, would miss tragically the delicate beauty of her every-day life, would fade under the ugly monotony of poverty.

But how could she say this to Mrs. Wayne, in her flat-heeled shoes and simple, boyish shirt and that twelfth-century saint's profile, of which so much might have been made by a clever woman?

At last she began, still smoothing her muff:

"Mrs. Wayne, I have brought up my daughter very simply. I don't at all approve of the extravagances of these modern girls, with their own motors and their own bills. Still, she has had a certain background. We must admit that marriage with your son on his income alone would mean a decrease in her material comforts."

Mrs. Wayne laughed.

"More than you know, probably."

This was candid, and Adelaide pressed on.

"Well is it wise or kind to make such a demand on a young creature when we know marriage is difficult at the best?" she asked.

Mrs. Wayne hesitated.

"You see, I have never seen your daughter, and I don't know what her
feeling for Pete may be."

"I'll answer both questions. She has a pleasant, romantic sentiment for Mr. Wayne - you know how one feels to one's first lover. She is a sweet, kind, unformed little girl, not heroic. But think of your own spirited son. Do you want this persistent, cruel responsibility for him?"

The question was an oratorical one, and Adelaide was astonished to find that Mrs. Wayne was answering it.

"Oh, yes," she said; "I want responsibility for Pete. It's exactly what he needs."

Adelaide stared at her in horror; she seemed the most unnatural mother in the world. She herself would fight to protect her daughter from the passive wear and tear of poverty; but she would have died to keep a son, if she had had one, from being driven into the active warfare of the support of a family.

In the pause that followed there was a ring at the bell, an argument with the servant, something that sounded like a scuffle, and then a young man strolled into the room. He was tall and beautifully dressed, - at least that was the first impression, - though, as a matter of fact, the clothes were of the cheapest ready-made variety. But nothing could look cheap or ill made on those splendid muscles. He wore a silk shirt, a flower in his buttonhole, a gray tie in which was a pearl as big as a pea, long patent-leather shoes with elaborate buff-colored tops; he carried a thin stick and a pair of new gloves in one hand, but the most conspicuous object in his dress was a brand-new, gray felt hat, with a rather wide brim, which he wore at an angle greater than Mr. Lanky attempted even at his jauntiest. His face was long and rather dark, and his eyes were a bright gray blue, under dark brows. He was scowling.

He strode into the middle of the room, and stood there, with his feet wide apart and his elbows slightly swaying. His hat was still on.

"Your servant said you couldn't see me," he said, with his back teeth set together, a method of enunciation that seemed to be habitual.

"Didn't want to would be truer, Marty," answered Mrs. Wayne, with a utmost good temper. "Still, as long as you're here, what do you want?"

Marty Burke didn't answer at once. He stood looking at Mrs. Wayne under his lowering brows; he had stopped swinging his elbows, and was now very slightly twitching his cane, as an evilly disposed cat will twitch the end of its tail.

Mrs. Farron watched him almost breathlessly. She was a little frightened, but the sensation was pleasurable. He was, she knew, the finest specimen of the human animal that she had ever seen.

"What do I want?" he said at length in a deep, rich

voice, shot here and there with strange nasal tones, and here and there with the remains of a brogue. "Well, I want that you should stop persecuting those poor kids."

"I persecuting them? Don't be absurd, Marty," answered Mrs. Wayne.

"Persecuting them; what else?" retorted Marty, fiercely. "What else is it? They wanting to get married, and you determined to send the boy up the river."

"I don't think we'll go over that again. I have a lady here on business."

"Oh, please don't mind me," said Mrs. Farron, settling back, and wriggling her hands contentedly into her muff. She rather expected the frivolous courage of her tone to draw the ire of Burke's glance upon her, but it did not.

"Cruel is what I call it," he went on. "She wants it, and he wants it, and her family wants it, and only you and the judge that you put up to opposing - "

"Her family do not want it. Her brother - "

"Her brother agrees with me. I was talking to him yesterday."

"Oh, that's why he has a black eye, is it?" said Mrs. Wayne.

"Black eyes or blue," said Marty, with a horizontal gesture of his hands, "her brother wants to see her married."

"Well, I don't," replied Mrs. Wayne, "at least not to this boy. I will never give my consent to putting a child of her age in the power of a degenerate little drunkard like that."

Mrs. Farron listened with all her ears. She did not think herself a prude, and only a moment before she had been accusing Mrs. Wayne of ignorance of the world; but never in all her life had she heard such words as were now freely exchanged between Burke and his hostess on the subject of the degree of consent that the girl in question had given to the advances of Burke's protege. She would have been as embarrassed as a girl if either of the disputants had been in the least aware of her presence. Once, she thought, Mrs. Wayne, for the sake of good manners, was on the point of turning to her and explaining the whole situation; but fortunately the exigencies of the dispute swept her on too fast. Adelaide was shocked, physically rather than morally, by the nakedness of their talk; but she did not want them to stop. She was fascinated by the spectacle of Marty Burke in action. She recognized at once that he was a dangerous man, not dangerous to female virtue, like all the other men to whom she had heard the term applied, but actually dangerous to life and property. She was not in the least afraid of him, but she knew he was a real danger. She enjoyed the knowledge. In most ways she was a woman timid in the face of physical danger, but she had never imagined being afraid of another human being. That much, perhaps, her sheltered training had done for her. "If she goes on irritating him like this he may murder us both," she thought. What she really meant was that he might murder Mrs. Wayne, but that, when he came to her and began to twist her neck, she would just say, "My dear man, don't be silly!" and he would stop.

In the meantime Burke was not so angry as he was affecting to be. Like most leaders of men, he had a strong dramatic instinct, and he had just led Mrs. Wayne to the climax of her just violence when his manner suddenly completely changed, and he said with the utmost good temper:

"And what do you think of my get-up, Mrs. Wayne? It's a new suit I have on, and a boutonniere." The change was so sudden that no one answered, and he went on, "It's clothes almost fit for a wedding that I'm wearing."

Mrs. Wayne understood him in a flash. She sprang to her feet.

"Marty Burke," she cried, "you don't mean to say you've got those two children married!"

"Not fifteen minutes ago, and I standing up with the groom." He smiled a smile of the wildest, most piercing sweetness - a smile so free and intense that it seemed impossible to connect it with anything but the consciousness of a pure heart. Mrs. Farron had never seen such a smile. "I thought I'd just drop around and give you the news," he said, and now for the first time took off his hat, displaying his crisp, black hair and round, pugnacious head. "Good morning, ladies." He bowed, and for an instant his glance rested on Mrs. Farron with an admiration too frank to be exactly offensive. He put his hat on his head, turned away, and made his exit, whistling.

He left behind him one person at least who had thoroughly enjoyed his triumph. To do her justice, however , Mrs. Farron was ashamed of her sympathy,

Alice Duer Miller

and she said gently to Mrs. Wayne:

"You think this marriage a very bad thing."

Mrs. Wayne pushed all her hair away from her temples.

"Oh, yes," she said, "it's a bad thing for the girl; but the worst is having Marty Burke put anything over. The district is absolutely under his thumb. I do wish, Mrs. Farron, you would get your husband to put the fear of God into him."

"My husband?"

"Yes; he works for your husband. He has charge of the loading and unloading of the trucks. He's proud of his job, and it gives him power over the laborers. He wouldn't want to lose his place. If your husband would send for him and say - " Mrs. Wayne hastily outlined the things Mr. Farron might say.

"He works for Vincent," Adelaide repeated. It seemed to her an absolutely stupendous coincidence, and her imagination pictured the clash between them - the effort of Vincent to put the fear of God into this man. Would he be able to? Which one would win? Never before had she doubted the superior power of her husband; now she did. "I think it would be hard to put the fear of God into that young man," she said aloud.

"I do wish Mr. Farron would try."

"Try," thought Adelaide, "and fail?" Could she stand that? Was her whole relation to Vincent about to be put to the test? What weapons had he against Marty

Burke? And if he had none, how stripped he would appear in her eyes!

"Won't you ask him, Mrs. Farron?"

Adelaide recoiled. She did not want to be the one to throw her glove among the lions.

"I don't think I understand well enough what it is you want. Why don't you ask him yourself?" She hesitated, knowing that no opportunity for this would offer unless she herself arranged it. "Why don't you come and dine with us to-night, and," she added more slowly, "bring your son?"

She had made the bait very attractive, and Mrs. Wayne did not refuse.

CHAPTER VI

As she drove home, Adelaide's whole being was stirred by the prospect of that conflict between Burke and her husband, and it was not until she saw Mathilde, pale with an hour of waiting, that she recalled the real object of her recent visit. Not, of course, that Adelaide was more interested in Marty Burke than in her daughter's future, but a titanic struggle fired her imagination more than a pitiful little romance. She felt a pang of self-reproach when she saw that Mr. Lanley had come to share the child's vigil, that he seemed to be suffering under an anxiety almost as keen as Mathilde's.

They did not have to question her; she threw out her hands, casting her muff from her as she did so.

"Oh," she said, "I'm a weak, soft-hearted creature! I've asked them both to dine tonight."

Mathilde flung herself into her mother's arms.

"O Mama, how marvelous you are!" she exclaimed.

Over her daughter's shoulder Adelaide noted her father's expression, a stiffening of the mouth and a brightening of the eyes.

"Your grandfather disapproves of me, Mathilde," she said.

"He couldn't be so unkind," returned the girl.

"After all," said Mr. Lanley, trying to induce a slight scowl, "if we are not going to consent to an engagement - "

"But you are," said Mathilde.

"We are not," said her mother; "but there is no reason why we should not meet and talk it over like sensible creatures - talk it over here" - Adelaide looked lovingly around her own subdued room - "instead of five stories up. For really - " She stopped, running her eyebrows together at the recollection.

"But the flat is rather - rather comfortable when you get there," said Mr. Lanley, suddenly becoming embarrassed over his choice of an adjective.

Adelaide looked at him sharply.

"Dear Papa," she asked, "since when have you become an admirer of painted shelves and dirty rugs? And I don't doubt," she added very gently, "that for the same money they could have found something quite tolerable in the country."

"Perhaps they don't want to live in the country," said Mr. Lanley, rather sharply: "I'm sure there is nothing that you'd hate more, Adelaide."

She opened her dark eyes.

"But I don't have to choose between squalor here or - "

"Squalor!" said Mr. Lanley. "Don't be ridiculous!"

Mathilde broke in gently at this point:

"I think you must have liked Mrs. Wayne, Mama, to ask her to dine."

Adelaide saw an opportunity to exercise one of her important talents.

"Yes," she said. "She has a certain naive friendliness. Of course I don't advocate, after fifty, dressing like an Eton boy; I always think an elderly face above a turned-down collar - "

"Mama," broke in Mathilde, quietly, "would you mind not talking of Mrs. Wayne like that? You know, she's Pete's mother."

Adelaide was really surprised.

"Why, my love," she answered, "I haven't said half the things I might say. I rather thought I was sparing your feelings. After all, when you see her, you will admit that she *does* dress like an Eton boy."

"She didn't when I saw her," said Mr. Lanley.

Adelaide turned to her father.

"Papa, I leave it to you. Did I say anything that should have wounded anybody's susceptibilities?"

Mr. Lanley hesitated.

"It was the tone Mathilde did not like, I think."

Adelaide raised her shoulders and looked beautifully hurt.

"My tone?" she wailed.

"It hurt me," said Mathilde, laying her little hand on her heart.

Mr. Lanley smiled at her, and then, springing up, kissed her tenderly on the forehead. He said it was time for him to be going on.

"You'll come to dinner to-night, Papa?"

Rather hastily, Mr. Lanley said no, he couldn't; he had an engagement. But his daughter did not let him get to the door.

"What are you going to do to-night, Papa?" she asked, firmly.

"There is a governor's meeting - "

"Two in a week, Papa?"

Suddenly Mr. Lanley dropped all pretense of not coming, and said he would be there at eight.

During the rest of the day Mathilde's heart never wholly regained its normal beat. Not only was she to see Pete again, and see him under the gaze of her united family, but she was to see this mother of his, whom he loved and admired so much. She pictured her as white-haired, benignant, brooding, the essential mother, with all her own mother's grace and charm left out, yet with these qualities not ill replaced by others which Mathilde sometimes dimly apprehended were lacking in her own beautiful parent. She looked at herself in the glass. "My son's wife," was the phrase in her mind.

On her way up-stairs to dress for dinner she tried to confide her anxieties to her mother.

"Mama," she said, "if you had a son, how would you feel toward the girl he wanted to marry?"

"Oh, I should think her a cat, of course," Adelaide answered; and added an instant later, "and I should probably be able to make him think so, too."

Mathilde sighed and went on up-stairs. Here she decided on an act of some insubordination. She would wear her best dress that evening, the dress which her mother considered too old for her. She did not want Pete's mother to think he had chosen a perfect baby.

Mr. Lanley, too, was a trifle nervous during the afternoon. He tried to say to himself that it was because the future of his darling little Mathilde was about to be settled. He shook his head, indicating that to settle the future of the young was a risky business; and then in a burst of self-knowledge he suddenly admitted that what was really making him nervous was the incident of the pier. If Mrs. Wayne referred to it, and of course there was no possible reason why she should not refer to it, Adelaide would never let him hear the last of it. It would be natural for Adelaide to think it queer that he hadn't told her about it. And the reason he hadn't told was perfectly clear: it was on that infernal pier that he had formed such an adverse opinion of Mrs. Wayne. But of course he did not wish to prejudice Adelaide; he wanted to leave her free to form her own opinions, and he was glad, excessively glad, that she had formed so favorable a one as to ask the woman to dinner. There was no question about his being glad; he surprised his servant by whistling as he put on his white waistcoat, and fastened the buckle rather more snugly than usual. Self-knowledge for the moment was not on hand.

He arrived at exactly the hour at which he always arrived, five minutes after eight, a moment not too early to embarrass the hostess and not too late to endanger the dinner.

No one was in the drawing-room but Mathilde and Farron. Adelaide, for one who had been almost perfectly brought up, did sometimes commit the fault of allowing her guests to wait for her.

"'Lo, my dear," said Mr. Lanley, kissing Mathilde. "What's that you have on? Never saw it before. Not so becoming as the dress you were wearing the last time I was here."

Mathilde felt that it would be almost easier to die immediately, and was revived only when she heard Farron saying:

"Oh, don't you like this? I was just thinking I had never seen Mathilde looking so well, in her rather more mature and subtle vein."

It was just as she wished to appear, but she glanced at her stepfather, disturbed by her constant suspicion that he read her heart more clearly than any one else, more clearly than she liked.

"How shockingly late they are!" said Adelaide, suddenly appearing in the utmost splendor. She moved about, kissing her father and arranging the chairs. "Do you know, Vin, why it is that Pringle likes to make the room look as if it were arranged for a funeral? Why do you suppose they don't come?"

"Any one who arrives after Adelaide is apt to be in wrong," observed her husband.

"Well, I think it's awfully incompetent always to be waiting for other people," she returned, just laying her hand an instant on his shoulder to indicate that he alone was privileged to make fun of her.

"That perhaps is what the Waynes think," he answered.

Mathilde's heart sank a little at this. She knew her mother did not like to be kept waiting for dinner.

"When I was a young man - " began Mr. Lanley.

"It was the custom," interrupted Adelaide in exactly the same tone, "for a hostess to be in her drawing-room at least five minutes before the hour set for the arrival of the guests."

"Adelaide," her father pleaded, "I don't talk like that; at least not often."

"You would, though, if you didn't have me to correct you," she retorted. "There's the bell at last; but it always takes people like that forever to get their wraps off."

"It's only ten minutes past eight," said Farron, and Mathilde blessed him with a look.

Mrs. Wayne came quickly into the room, so fast that her dress floated behind her; she was in black and very grand. No one would have supposed that she had murmured to Pete just before the drawing-room door was opened, "I hope they haven't run in any old relations on us."

"I'm afraid I'm late," she began.

"She always is," Pete murmured to Mathilde as he took her hand and quite openly squeezed it, and then, before Adelaide had time for the rather casual introduction she had planned, he himself put the hand he was holding into his mother's. "This is my girl, Mother," he said. They smiled at each other. Mathilde tried to say something. Mrs. Wayne stooped and kissed her. Mr. Lanley was obviously affected. Adelaide wasn't going to have any scene like that.

"Late?" she said, as if not an instant had passed since Mrs. Wayne's entrance. "Oh, no, you're not late; exactly on time, I think. I'm only just down myself. Isn't that true, Vincent?"

Vincent was studying Mrs. Wayne, and withdrew his eyes slowly. But Adelaide's object was accomplished: no public betrothal had taken place.

Pringle announced dinner. Mr. Lanley, rather to his own surprise, found that he was insisting on giving Mrs. Wayne his arm; he was not so angry at her as he had supposed. He did not think her offensive or unfeminine or half baked or socialistic or any of the things he had been saying to himself at lengthening intervals for the last twenty-four hours.

Pete saw an opportunity, and tucked Mathilde's hand within his own arm, nipping it closely to his heart.

The very instant they were at table Adelaide looked down the alley between the candles, for the low, golden dish of hot-house fruit did not obstruct her view of Vincent, and said:

"Why have you never told me about Marty Burke?"

"Who's he?" asked Mr. Lanley, quickly, for he had been trying to start a little conversational hare of his own, just to keep the conversation away from the water-front.

"He's a splendid young super-tough in my employ," said Vincent. "What do you know about him, Adelaide?"

The guarded surprise in his tone stimulated her.

"Oh, I know all about him - as much, that is, as one ever can of a stupendous natural phenomenon."

"Where did you hear of him?"

"Hear of him? I've seen him. I saw him this morning at Mrs. Wayne's. He just dropped in while I was there and, metaphorically speaking, dragged us about by the hair of our heads."

"Some women, I believe, confess to enjoying that sensation," Vincent observed.

"Yes, it's exciting," answered his wife.

"It's an easy excitement to attain."

"Oh, one wants it done in good style."

Something so stimulating that it was almost hostile flashed through the interchange.

Mathilde murmured to Pete:

"Who are they talking about?"

"A mixture of Alcibiades and *Bill Sykes*," said Adelaide, catching the low tone, as she always did.

"He's the district leader and a very bad influence," said Mrs. Wayne.

"He's a champion middle-weight boxer," said Pete.

"He's the head of my stevedores," said Farron.

"O Mr. Farron," Mrs. Wayne exclaimed, "I do wish you would use your influence over him."

"My influence? It consists of paying him eighty-five dollars a month and giving him a box of cigars at Christmas."

"Don't you think you could tone him down?" pleaded Mrs. Wayne. "He does so much harm."

"But I don't want him toned down. His value to me is his being just as he is. He's a myth, a hero, a power on the water-front, and I employ him."

"You employ him, but do you control him?" asked Adelaide, languidly, and yet with a certain emphasis.

Her husband glanced at her.

"What is it you want, Adelaide?" he said.

She gave a little laugh.

"Oh, I want nothing. It's Mrs. Wayne who wants you to do something - rather difficult, too, I should imagine."

He turned gravely to their guest.

"What is it you want, Mrs. Wayne?"

Mrs. Wayne considered an instant, and as she was about to find words for her request her son spoke:

"She'll tell you after dinner."

"Pete, I wasn't going to tell the story," his mother put in protestingly. "You really do me injustice at times."

Adelaide, remembering the conversation of the morning, wondered whether he did. She felt grateful to him for wishing to spare Mathilde the hearing of such a story, and she turned to him with a caressing graciousness in which she was extremely at her ease. Mathilde, recognizing that her mother was pleased, though not being very clear why, could not resist joining in their conversation; and Mrs. Wayne was thus given an opportunity of murmuring the unfortunate Anita's story into Vincent's ear.

Adelaide, holding Pete with a flattering gaze, seeming to drink in every word he was saying, heard Mrs. Wayne finish and heard Vincent say:

"And you think you can get it annulled if only Burke doesn't interfere?"

"Yes, if he doesn't get hold of the boy and tell him that his dignity as a man is involved."

Adelaide withdrew her gaze from Pete and fixed it on Vincent. Was he going to accept that challenge? She wanted him to, and yet she thought he would be defeated, and she did not want him to be defeated. She waited almost breathless.

"Well, I'll see what I can do," he said. This was an acceptance. This from Vincent meant that the matter, as far as he was concerned, was settled.

"You two plotters!" exclaimed Adelaide. "For my part, I'm on Marty Burke's side. I hate to see wild creatures in cages."

"Dangerous to side with wild beasts," observed Vincent.

"Why?"

"They get the worst of it in the long run."

Adelaide dropped her eyes. It was exactly the right answer. For a moment she felt his complete supremacy. Then another thought shot through her mind: it was exactly the right answer if he could make it good.

In the meantime Mr. Lanley began to grow dissatisfied with the prolonged role of spectator. He preferred danger to oblivion; and turning to Mrs. Wayne, he said, with his politest smile:

"How are the bridges?"

"Oh, dear," she answered, "I must have been terribly tactless - to make you so angry."

Mr. Lanley drew himself up.

"I was not angry," he said.

She looked at him with a sort of gentle wonder.

"You gave me the impression of being."

The very temperateness of the reply made him see that he had been inaccurate.

"Of course I was angry," he said. "What I mean is that I don't understand why I was."

Meantime, on the opposite side of the table, Mathilde and Pete were equally immersed, murmuring sentences of the profoundest meaning behind faces which they felt were mask-like.

Farron looked down the table at his wife. Why, he wondered, did she want to tease him to-night, of all nights in his life?

When they came out of the dining-room Pete said to Mathilde with the utmost clearness:

"And what was that magazine you spoke of?"

She had spoken of no magazine, but she caught the idea, the clever, rather wicked idea. He made her work her mind almost too fast sometimes, but she enjoyed it.

"Wasn't it this?" she asked, with a beating heart.

They sat down on the sofa and bent their heads over it with student-like absorption.

"I haven't any idea what it is," she whispered.

"Oh, well, I suppose there's something or other in it."

"I think your mother is perfectly wonderful - wonderful."

"I love you so."

The older people took a little longer to settle down. Mr. Lanley stood on the hearth-rug, with a cigar in his mouth and his head thrown very far back. Adelaide sank into a chair, looking, as she often did, as if she had just been brilliantly well posed for a photograph. Farron was silent. Mrs. Wayne sat, as she had a bad habit of doing, on one foot. The two groups were sufficiently separated for distinct conversations.

"Is this a conference?" asked Farron.

Mrs. Wayne made it so by her reply.

"The whole question is, Are they really in love? At least, that's my view."

"In love!" Adelaide twisted her shoulders. "What can they know of it for another ten years? You must have some character, some knowledge to fall in love. And these babes -"

"No," said Mr. Lanley, stoutly; "you're all wrong, Adelaide. It's first love that matters - *Romeo* and *Juliet*, you know. Afterward we all get hardened and world-worn and cynical and material." He stopped short in his eloquence at the thought that Mrs. Wayne was quite obviously not hardened or world-worn or cynical or material. "By Jove!" he thought to himself, "that's it. The woman's spirit is as fresh as a girl's." He had by this time utterly forgotten what he had meant to say.

Adelaide turned to her husband.

"Do you think they are in love, Vin?"

Vincent looked at her for a second, and then he nodded two or three times.

Though no one at once recognized the fact, the engagement was settled at that moment.

It seemed obvious that Mr. Lanley should take the Waynes home in his car. Mrs. Wayne, who had prepared for walking with overshoes and with pins for her trailing skirt, did not seem too enthusiastic at the suggestion. She stood a moment on the step and looked at the sky, where Orion, like a banner, was hung across the easterly opening of the side street.

"It's a lovely night," she said.

It was Pete who drew her into the car. Her reluctance deprived Mr. Lanley of the delight of bestowing a benefit, but gave him a faint sense of capture.

In the drawing-room Mathilde was looking from one to the other of her natural guardians, like a well-trained puppy who wants to be fed. She wanted Pete praised. Instead, Adelaide said:

"Really, papa is growing too secretive! Do you know, Vin, he and Mrs. Wayne quarreled like mad last evening, and he never told me a word about it!"

"How do you know?"

"Oh, I heard them trying to smooth it out at dinner."

"O Mama," wailed Mathilde, between admiration and complaint, "you hear everything!"

"Certainly, I do," Adelaide returned lightly. "Yes, and I heard you, too, and understood everything that you meant."

Vincent couldn't help smiling at his stepdaughter's horrified look.

"What a brute you are, Adelaide!" he said.

"Oh, my dear, you're much worse," she retorted. "You don't have to overhear. You just read the human heart by some black magic of your own. That's really more cruel than my gross methods."

"Well, Mathilde," said Farron, "as a reader of the human heart, I want to tell you that I approve of the young man. He has a fine, delicate touch on life, which, I am inclined to think, goes only with a good deal of strength."

Mathilde blinked her eyes. Gratitude and delight had brought tears to them.

"He thinks you're wonderful, Mr. Farron," she answered a little huskily.

"Better and better," answered Vincent, and he held out his hand for a letter that Pringle was bringing to him on a tray.

"What's that?" asked Adelaide. One of the first things she had impressed on Joe Severance was that he must never inquire about her mail; but she always asked Farron about his.

He seemed to be thinking and didn't answer her.

Mathilde, now simply insatiable, pressed nearer to him and asked:

"And what do you think of Mrs. Wayne?"

He raised his eyes from the envelope, and answered with a certain absence of tone:

"I thought she was an elderly wood-nymph."

Adelaide glanced over his shoulder , and, seeing that

the letter had a printed address in the corner, lost interest.

"You may shut the house, Pringle," she said.

Alice Duer Miller

CHAPTER VII

Pringle, the last servant up, was soon heard discreetly drawing bolts and turning out electric lights. Mathilde went straight up-stairs without even an attempt at drawing her mother into an evening gossip. She was aware of being tired after two nights rendered almost sleepless by her awareness of joy. She went to her room and shut the door. Her bed was piled high with extra covers, soft, light blankets and a down coverlet covered with pink silk. She took a certain hygienic pride in the extent to which she always opened her bedroom windows even when, as at present, the night was bitterly cold. In the morning she ran, huddling on her dressing-gown, into a heated bathroom, and when she emerged from this, the maid had always lighted her fire, and laid her breakfast-tray close to the blaze. To-night, when she went to open her window, she noticed that the houses opposite had lost courage and showed only cracks. She stood a second looking up at the stars, twinkling with tiny blue rays through the clear air. By turning her head to the west she could look down on the park, with its surface of bare, blurred tree-branches pierced by rows of lights. The familiar sight suddenly seemed to her almost intolerably beautiful. "Oh, I love him so much!" she said to herself, and her lips actually whispered the words, "so much! so much!"

She threw the window high as a reproof of those

shivers across the way, and, jumping into bed, hastily sandwiched her small body between the warm bedclothes. She was almost instantly asleep.

Overhead the faint, but heavy, footfall of Pringle ceased. The house was silent; the city had become so. An occasional Madison Avenue car could be heard ringing along the cold rails, or rhythmically bounding down hill on a flat wheel. Once some distance away came the long, continuous complaint of the siren of a fire-engine and the bells and gongs of its comrades; and then a young man went past, whistling with the purest accuracy of time and tune the air to which he had just been dancing.

At half-past five the kitchen-maid, a young Swede who feared not God, neither regarded man, but lived in absolute subjection to the cook, to whom, unknown to any one else, she every morning carried up breakfast, was stealing down with a candle in her hand. Her senses were alert, for a friend of hers had been strangled by burglars in similar circumstances, and she had never overcome her own terror of the cold, dark house in these early hours of a winter morning.

She went down not the back stairs, for Mr. Pringle objected that she woke him as she passed, whereas the carpet on the front stairs was so thick that there wasn't the least chance of waking the family. As she passed Mrs. Farron's room she was surprised to see a fine crack of light coming from under it. She paused, wondering if she was going to be caught, and if she had better run back and take to the back stairs despite Pringle's well-earned rest; and as she hesitated she heard a sob, then another - wild, hysterical sobs. The girl looked startled and then went on, shaking her head.

What people like that had to cry about beat her. But she was glad, because she knew such a splendid bit of news would soften the heart of the cook when she took up her breakfast.

By five o'clock it seemed to Adelaide that a whole eternity had passed and that another was ahead of her, that this night would never end.

When they went up-stairs, while she was brushing her hair - her hair rewarded brushing, for it was fine and long and took a polish like bronze - she had wandered into Vincent's room to discuss with him the question of her father's secretiveness about Mrs. Wayne. It was not, she explained, standing in front of his fire, that she suspected anything, but that it was so unfriendly: it deprived one of so much legitimate amusement if one's own family practised that kind of reserve. Her just anger kept her from observing Farron very closely. As she talked she laid her brush on the mantelpiece, and as she did so she knocked down the letter that had come for him just before they went up-stairs. She stooped, and picked it up without attention, and stood holding it; she gesticulated a little with it as she repeated, for her own amusement rather than for Vincent's, phrases she had caught at dinner.

The horror to Farron of seeing her standing there chattering, with that death-dealing letter in her hand, suddenly and illogically broke down his resolution of silence. It was cruel, and though he might have denied himself her help, he could not endure cruelty.

"Adelaide," he said in a tone that drove every other sensation away - "Adelaide, that letter. No, don't read it." He took it from her and laid it on his dressing-table. "My dear love, it has very bad news in it."

"There *has* been something, then?"

"Yes. I have been worried about my health for some time. This letter tells me the worst is true. Well, my dear, we did not enter matrimony with the idea that either of us was immortal."

But that was his last effort to be superior to the crisis, to pretend that the bitterness of death was any less to him than to any other human creature, to conceal that he needed help, all the help that he could get.

And Adelaide gave him help. Artificial as she often was in daily contact, in a moment like this she was splendidly, almost primitively real. She did not conceal her own passionate despair, her conviction that her life couldn't go on without his; she did not curb her desire to know every detail on which his opinion and his doctor's had been founded; she clung to him and wept, refusing to let him discuss business arrangements, in which for some reason he seemed to find a certain respite; and yet with it all, she gave him strength, the sense that he had an indissoluble and loyal companion in the losing fight that lay before him.

Once she was aware of thinking: "Oh, why did he tell me to-night? Things are so terrible by night," but it was only a second before she put such a thought away from her. What had these nights been to him? The night when she had found his light burning so late, and other nights when he had probably denied himself the consolation of reading for fear of rousing her suspicions. She did not attempt to pity or advise him, she did not treat him as a mixture of child and idiot, as affection so often treats illness. She simply gave him her love.

Toward morning he fell asleep in her arms, and then she stole back to her own room. There everything was unchanged, the light still burning, her satin slippers stepping on each other just as she had left them. She looked at herself in the glass; she did not look so very different. A headache had often ravaged her appearance more.

She had always thought herself a coward, she feared death with a terrible repugnance; but now she found, to her surprise, that she would have light-heartedly changed places with her husband. She had much more courage to die than to watch him die - to watch Vincent die, to see him day by day grow weak and pitiful. That was what was intolerable. If he would only die now, to-night, or if she could! It was at this moment that the kitchen maid had heard her sobbing.

Because there was nothing else to do, she got into bed, and lay there staring at the electric light, which she had forgotten to put out. Toward seven she got up and gave orders that Mr. Farron was not to be disturbed, that the house was to be kept quiet. Strange, she thought, that he could sleep like an exhausted child, while she, awake, was a mass of pain. Her heart ached, her eyes burned, her very body felt sore. She arranged for his sleep, but she wanted him to wake up; she begrudged every moment of his absence. Alas! she thought, how long would she continue to do so?

Yet with her suffering came a wonderful ease, an ability to deal with the details of life. When at eight o'clock her maid came in and, pulling the curtains, exclaimed with Gallic candor, "Oh, comme madame a mauvaise mine ce matin!" she smiled at her with unusual gentleness. Later, when Mathilde came down at her accustomed hour, and lying across the foot of her mother's bed, began to read her scraps of the morning paper, Adelaide felt a rush of tenderness for the child, who was so unaware of the hideous bargain life really was. Surprising as it was, she found she could talk more easily than usual and with a more undivided attention, though everything they said was trivial enough.

Then suddenly her heart stood still, for the door opened, and Vincent, in his dressing-gown, came in. He had evidently had his bath, for his hair was wet and shiny. Thank God! he showed no signs of defeat!

"Oh," cried Mathilde, jumping up, "I thought Mr. Farron had gone down-town ages ago."

"He overslept," said Adelaide.

"I had an excellent night," he answered, and she knew he looked at her to discover that she had not.

"I'll go," said Mathilde; but with unusual sharpness they both turned to her and said simultaneously, "No, no; stay." They knew no better than she did why they were so eager to keep her.

"Are you going down-town, Vin?" Adelaide asked, and her voice shook a little on the question; she was so eager that he should not institute any change in his routine so soon.

"Of course," he answered.

They looked at each other, yet their look said nothing in particular. Presently he said:

"I wonder if I might have breakfast in here. I'll go and shave if you'll order it; and don't let Mathilde go. I have something to say to her."

When he was gone, Mathilde went and stood at the window, looking out, and tying knots in the window-shade's cord. It was a trick Adelaide had always objected to, and she was quite surprised to hear herself saying now, just as usual:

"Mathilde, don't tie knots in that cord."

Mathilde threw it from her as one whose mind was engaged on higher things.

"You know," she observed, "I believe I'm only just beginning to appreciate Mr. Farron. He's so wise. I see what you meant about his being strong, and he's so clever. He knows just what you're thinking all the time. Isn't it nice that he likes Pete? Did he say anything more about him after you went up-stairs? I mean, he really does like him, doesn't he? He doesn't say that just to please me?"

Presently Vincent came back fully dressed and sat down to his breakfast. Oddly enough, there was a spirit of real gaiety in the air.

"What was it you were going to say to me?" Mathilde asked greedily. Farron looked at her blankly. Adelaide knew that he had quite forgotten the phrase, but he concealed the fact by not allowing the least illumination of his expression as he remembered.

"Oh, yes," he said. "I wish to correct myself. I told you that Mrs. Wayne was an elderly wood-nymph; but I was wrong. Of course the truth is that she's a very young witch."

Mathilde laughed, but not whole-heartedly. She had already identified herself so much with the Waynes that she could not take them quite in this tone of impersonality.

Farron threw down his napkin, stood up, pulled down his waistcoat.

"I must be off," he said. He went and kissed his wife. Both had to nerve themselves for that.

She held his arm in both her hands, feeling it solid, real, and as hard as iron.

"You'll be up-town early?"

"I've a busy day."

"By four?"

"I'll telephone." She loved him for refusing to yield to her just at this moment of all moments. Some men, she thought, would have hidden their own self-pity under the excuse of the necessity of being kind to her.

She was to lunch out with a few critical contemporaries. She was horrified when she looked at herself by morning light. Her skin had an ivory hue, and there were many fine wrinkles about her eyes. She began to repair these damages with the utmost frankness, talking meantime to Mathilde and the maid. She swept her whole face with a white lotion, rouged lightly, but to her very eyelids, touched a red pencil to her lips, all with discretion. The result was satisfactory. The improvement in her appearance made her feel braver. She couldn't have faced these people - she did not know whether to think of them as intimate enemies or hostile friends - if she had been looking anything but her best.

But they were just what she needed; they would be hard and amusing and keep her at some tension. She thought rather crossly that she could not sit through a meal at home and listen to Mathilde rambling on about love and Mr. Farron.

She was inexcusably late, and they had sat down to luncheon - three men and two women - by the time she arrived. They had all been, or had wanted to go, to an auction sale of *objets d'art* that had taken place the night before. They were discussing it, praising their own purchases, and decrying the value of everybody else's when Adelaide came in.

"Oh, Adelaide," said her hostess, "we were just wondering what you paid originally for your tapestry."

"The one in the hall?"

"No, the one with the Turk in it."

"I haven't an idea, - " Adelaide was distinctly languid, - "I got it from my grandfather."

"Wouldn't you know she'd say that?" exclaimed one of

the women. "Not that I deny it's true; only, you know, Adelaide, whenever you do want to throw a veil over one of your pieces, you always call on the prestige of your ancestors."

Adelaide raised her eyebrows.

"Really," she answered, "there isn't anything so very conspicuous about having had a grandfather."

"No," her hostess echoed, "even I, so well and favorably known for my vulgarity - even *I* had a grandfather."

"But he wasn't a connoisseur in tapestries, Minnie darling."

"No, but he was in pigs, the dear vulgarian."

"True vulgarity," said one of the men, "vulgarity in the best sense, I mean, should betray no consciousness of its own existence. Only thus can it be really great."

"Oh, Minnie's vulgarity is just artificial, assumed because she found it worked so well."

"Surely you accord her some natural talent along those lines."

"I suspect her secret mind is refined."

"Oh, that's not fair. Vulgar is as vulgar does."

Adelaide stood up, pushing back her chair. She found them utterly intolerable. Besides, as they talked she had suddenly seen clearly that she must herself speak to Vincent's doctor without an instant's delay. "I have to telephone, Minnie," she said, and swept out of the room. She never returned.

"Not one of the perfect lady's golden days, I should say," said one of the men, raising his eyebrows. "I wonder what's gone wrong?"

"Can Vincent have been straying from the straight and narrow?"

"Something wrong. I could tell by her looks."

"Ah, my dear, I'm afraid her looks is what's wrong."

Adelaide meantime was in her motor on her way to the doctor's office. He had given up his sacred lunch-hour in response to her imperious demand and to his own intense pity for her sorrow.

He did not know her, but he had had her pointed out to him, and though he recognized the unreason of such an attitude, he was aware that her great beauty dramatized her suffering, so that his pity for her was uncommonly alive.

He was a young man, with a finely cut face and a blond complexion. His pity was visible, quivering a little under his mask of impassivity. Adelaide's first thought on seeing him was, "Good Heavens! another man to be emotionally calmed before I can get at the truth!" She had to be tactful, to let him see that she was not going to make a scene. She knew that he felt it himself, but she was not grateful to him. What business had he to feel it? His feeling was an added burden, and she felt that she had enough to carry.

He did not make the mistake, however, of expressing his sympathy verbally. His answers were as cold and clear as she could wish. She questioned him on the chances of an operation. He could not reduce his judgment to a mathematical one; he was inclined to advocate an operation on psychological grounds, he said.

"It keeps up the patient's courage to know something is being done." He added, "That will be your work, Mrs. Farron, to keep his courage up."

Most women like to know they had their part to play, but Adelaide shook her head quickly.

"I would so much rather go through it myself!" she cried.

"Naturally, naturally," he agreed, without getting the full passion of her cry.

She stood up.

"Oh," she said, "if it could only be kill or cure!"

He glanced at her.

"We have hardly reached that point yet," he answered.

She went away dissatisfied. He had answered every question, he had even encouraged her to hope a little more than her interpretation of what Vincent said had allowed her; but as she drove away she knew he had failed her. For she had gone to him in order to have Vincent presented to her as a hero, as a man who had looked upon the face of death without a quiver.

Instead, he had been presented to her as a patient, just one of the long procession that passed through that office. The doctor had said nothing to contradict the heroic picture, but he had said nothing to contribute to it. And surely, if Farron had stood out in his calmness and courage above all other men, the doctor would have mentioned it, couldn't have helped doing so; he certainly would not have spent so much time in telling her how she was to guard and encourage him. To the doctor he was only a patient, a pitiful human being, a victim of mortality. Was that what he was going to become in her eyes, too?

At four she drove down-town to his office. He came out with another man; they stood a moment on the steps talking and smiling. Then he drew his friend to the car window and introduced him to Adelaide. The man took off his hat.

"I was just telling your husband, Mrs. Farron, that I've been looking at offices in this building. By the spring he and I will be neighbors."

Adelaide just shut her eyes, and did not open them again until Vincent had got in beside her and she felt his arm about her shoulder.

"My poor darling!" he said. "What you need is to go home and get some sleep." It was said in his old, cherishing tone, and she, leaning back, with her head against the point of his shoulder, felt that, black as it was, life for the first time since the night before had assumed its normal aspect again.

CHAPTER VIII

The morning after their drive up-town Vincent told his wife that all his arrangements were made to go to the hospital that night, and to be operated upon the next day. She reproached him for having made his decision without consulting her, but she loved him for his proud independence.

Somehow this second day under the shadow of death was less terrible than the first. Vincent stayed up-town, and was very natural and very busy. He saw a few people, - men who owed him money, his lawyer, his partner, - but most of the time he and Adelaide sat together in his study, as they had sat on many other holidays. He insisted on going alone to the hospital, although she was to be in the building during the operation.

Mathilde had been told, and inexperienced in disaster, she had felt convinced that the outcome couldn't be fatal, yet despite her conviction that people did not really die, she was aware of a shyness and awkwardness in the tragic situation.

Mr. Lanley had been told, and his attitude was just the opposite. To him it seemed absolutely certain that Farron would die, - every one did, - but he had for some time been aware of a growing hardness on his part toward the death of other people, as if he were thus preparing himself for his own.

"Poor Vincent!" he said to himself. "Hard luck at his age, when an old man like me is left." But this was not quite honest. In his heart he felt there was nothing unnatural in Vincent's being taken or in his being left.

As usual in a crisis, Adelaide's behavior was perfect. She contrived to make her husband feel every instant the depth, the strength, the passion of her love for him without allowing it to add to the weight he was already carrying. Alone together, he and she had flashes of real gaiety, sometimes not very far from tears.

To Mathilde the brisk naturalness of her mother's manner was a source of comfort. All the day the girl suffered from a sense of strangeness and isolation, and a fear of doing or saying something unsuitable - something either too special or too every-day. She longed to evince sympathy for Mr. Farron, but was afraid that, if she did, it would be like intimating that he was as good as dead. She was caught between the negative danger of seeming indifferent and the positive one of being tactless.

As soon as Vincent had left the house, Adelaide's thought turned to her daughter. He had gone about six o'clock. He and she had been sitting by his study fire when Pringle announced that the motor was waiting. Vincent got up quietly, and so did she. They stood with their arms about each other, as if they meant never to forget the sense of that contact; and then without any protest they went down-stairs together.

In the hall he had shaken hands with Mr. Lanley and

had kissed Mathilde, who, do what she would, couldn't help choking a little. All this time Adelaide stood on the stairs, very erect, with one hand on the stair-rail and one on the wall, not only her eyes, but her whole face, radiating an uplifted peace. So angelic and majestic did she seem that Mathilde, looking up at her, would hardly have been surprised if she had floated out into space from her vantage-ground on the staircase.

Then Farron lit a last cigar, gave a quick, steady glance at his wife, and went out. The front door ended the incident as sharply as a shot would have done.

It was then that Mathilde expected to see her mother break down. Under all her sympathy there was a faint human curiosity as to how people contrived to live through such crises. If Pete were on the brink of death, she thought that she would go mad: but, then, she and Pete were not a middle-aged married couple; they were young, and new to love.

They all went into the drawing-room, Adelaide the calmest of the three.

"I wonder," she said, "if you two would mind dining a little earlier than usual. I might sleep if I could get to bed early, and I must be at the hospital before eight."

Mr. Lanley agreed a little more quickly than it was his habit to speak.

"O Mama, I think you're so marvelous!" said Mathilde, and touched at her own words, she burst into tears. Her mother put her arm about her, and Mr. Lanley patted her shoulder - his sovereign care.

Alice Duer Miller

"There, there, my dear," he murmured, "you must not cry. You know Vincent has a very good chance, a very good chance."

The assumption that he hadn't was just the one Mathilde did not want to appear to make. Her mother saw this and said gently:

"She's overstrained, that's all."

The girl wiped her eyes.

"I'm ashamed, when you are so calm and wonderful."

"I'm not wonderful," said her mother. "I have no wish to cry. I'm beyond it. Other people's trouble often makes us behave more emotionally than our own. If it were your Pete, I should be in tears." She smiled, and looked across the girl's head at Mr. Lanley. "She would like to see him, Papa. Telephone Pete Wayne, will you, and ask him to come and see her this evening? You'll be here, won't you?"

Mr. Lanley nodded without cordiality; he did not approve of encouraging the affair unnecessarily.

"How kind you are, Mama!" exclaimed Mathilde, almost inaudibly. It was just what she wanted, just what she had been wanting all day, to see her own man, to assure herself, since death was seen to be hot on the trail of all mortals, that he and she were not wasting their brief time in separation.

"We might take a turn in the motor," said Mr. Lanley, thinking that Mrs. Wayne might enjoy that.

"It would do you both good."

"And leave you alone, Mama?"

"It's what I really want, dear."

The plan did not fulfil itself quite as Mr. Lanley had imagined. Mrs. Wayne was out at some sort of meeting. They waited a moment for Pete. Mathilde fixed her eyes on the lighted doorway, and said to herself that in a few seconds the thing of all others that she desired would happen - he would come through it. And almost at once he did, looking particularly young and alive; so that, as he jumped in beside her on the back seat, both her hands went out and caught his arm and clung to him. Her realization of mortality had been so acute that she felt as if he had been restored to her from the dead. She told him the horrors of the day. Particularly, she wanted to share with him her gratitude for her mother's almost magic kindness.

"I wanted you so much, Pete," she whispered; "but I thought it would be heartless even to suggest my having wishes at such a time. And then for her to think of it herself - "

"It means they are not really going to oppose our marriage."

They talked about their marriage and the twenty or thirty years of joy which they might reasonably hope to snatch from life.

"Think of it," he said - "twenty or thirty years, longer than either of us have lived."

Alice Duer Miller

"If I could have five years, even one year, with you, I think I could bear to die; but not now, Pete."

In the meantime Mr. Lanley, alone on the front seat, for he had left his chauffeur at home, was driving north along the Hudson and saying to himself:

"Sixty-four. Well, I may be able to knock out ten or twelve pretty satisfactory years. On the other hand, might die to-morrow; hope I don't, though. As long as I can drive a car and everything goes well with Adelaide and this child, I'd be content to live my full time - and a little bit more. Not many men are healthier than I am. Poor Vincent! A good deal more to live for than I have, most people would say; but I don't know that he enjoys it any more than I do." Turning his head a little, he shouted over his shoulder to Pete, "Sorry your mother couldn't come."

Mathilde made a hasty effort to withdraw her hands; but Wayne, more practical, understanding better the limits put upon a driver, held them tightly as he answered in a civil tone: "Yes, she would have enjoyed this."

"She must come some other time," shouted Mr. Lanley, and reflected that it was not always necessary to bring the young people with you.

"You know, he could not possibly have turned enough to see," Pete whispered reprovingly to Mathilde.

"I suppose not; and yet it seemed so queer to be talking to my grandfather with - "

" You must try and adapt yourself to your

environment," he returned, and put his arm about her.

The cold of the last few days had given place to a thaw. The melting ice in the river was streaked in strange curves, and the bare trees along the straight heights of the Palisades were blurred by a faint bluish mist, out of which white lights and yellow ones peered like eyes.

"Doesn't it seem cruel to be so happy when Mama and poor Mr. Farron - " Mathilde began.

"It's the only lesson to learn," he answered - "to be happy while we are young and together."

About ten o'clock Mr. Lanley left her at home, and she tiptoed up-stairs and hardly dared to draw breath as she undressed for fear she might wake her unhappy mother on the floor below her.

She had resolved to wake early, to breakfast with her mother, to ask to be allowed to accompany her to the hospital; but it was nine o'clock when she was awakened by her maid's coming in with her breakfast and the announcement not only that Mrs. Farron had been gone for more than an hour, but that there had already been good news from the hospital.

"Il parait que monsieur est tres fort," she said, with that absolute neutrality of accent that sounds in Anglo-Saxon ears almost like a complaint.

Adelaide had been in no need of companionship. She was perfectly able to go through her day. It seemed as if her soul, with a soul's capacity for suffering, had suddenly withdrawn from her body, had retreated into some unknown fortress, and left in its place a hard, trivial, practical intelligence which tossed off plan after plan for the future detail of life. As she drove from her house to the hospital she arranged how she would apportion the household in case of a prolonged illness, where she would put the nurses. Nor was she less clear as to what should be done in case of Vincent's death. The whole thing unrolled before her like a panorama.

At the hospital, after a little delay, she was guided to Vincent's own room, recently deserted. A nurse came to tell her that all was going well; Mr. Farron had had a good night, and was taking the anesthetic nicely. Adelaide found the young woman's manner offensively encouraging, and received the news with an insolent reserve.

"That girl is too wildly, spiritually bright," she said to herself. But no manner would have pleased her.

Left alone, she sat down in a rocking-chair near the window. Vincent's bag stood in the corner, his brushes were on the dressing-table, his tie hung on the electric light. Immortal trifles, she thought, that might be in existence for years.

She began poignantly to regret that she had not insisted on seeing him again that morning. She had thought only of what was easiest for him. She ought to have thought of herself, of what would make it possible for her to go on living without him. If she could have seen him again, he might have given her some precept, some master word, by which she could have guided her life. She would have welcomed something imprisoning and safe. It was cruel of him, she thought, to toss her out like this, rudderless and alone. She wondered what he would have given her as a commandment, and remembered suddenly the apocryphal last words which Vincent was fond of attributing to George Washington, "Never trust a nigger with a gun." She found herself smiling over them. Vincent was more likely to have quoted the apparition's advice to Macbeth: "Be bloody, bold, and resolute." That would have been his motto for himself, but not for her. What was the principle by which he infallibly guided her?

How could he have left her so spiritually unprovided for? She felt imposed upon, deserted. The busily planning little mind that had suddenly taken possession of her could not help her in the larger aspects of her existence. It would be much simpler, she thought, to die than to attempt life again without Vincent.

She went to the window and looked out at the roofs of neighboring houses, a disordered conglomeration of water-tanks and skylights and chimney-pots. Then nearer, almost under her feet, she looked into a court-yard of the hospital and saw a pale, emaciated man in a wheel-chair. She drew back as if it were something indecent. Would Vincent ever become like that? she thought. If so, she would rather he died now under the anesthetic.

A little while later the nurse came in, and said almost sternly that Dr. Crew had sent her to tell Mrs. Farron that the conditions seemed extremely favorable, and that all immediate danger was over.

"You mean," said Adelaide, fiercely, "that Mr. Farron will live?"

"I certainly inferred that to be the doctor's meaning,"

answered the nurse. "But here is the assistant, Dr. Withers."

Dr. Withers, bringing with him an intolerable smell of disinfectants and chloroform, hurried in, with his hair mussed from the haste with which he had removed his operating-garments. He had small, bright, brown eyes, with little lines about them that seemed to suggest humor, but actually indicated that he buoyed up his life not by exaltation of himself, but by half-laughing depreciation of every one else.

"I thought you'd be glad to know, Mrs. Farron," he said, "that any danger that may have existed is now over. Your husband - "

"That *may* have existed," cried Adelaide. "Do you mean to say there hasn't been any real danger?"

The young doctor's eyes twinkled.

"An operation even in the best hands is always a danger," he replied.

"But you mean there was no other?" Adelaide asked, aware of a growing coldness about her hands and feet.

Withers looked as just as Aristides.

"It was probably wise to operate," he said. "Your husband ought to be up and about in three weeks."

Everything grew black and rotatory before Adelaide's eyes, and she sank slowly forward into the young doctor's arms.

As he laid her on the bed, he glanced whimsically at the nurse and shook his head.

But she made no response, an omission which may not have meant loyalty to Dr. Crew so much as unwillingness to support Dr. Withers.

Adelaide returned to consciousness only in time to be hurried away to make room for Vincent. His long, limp figure was carried past her in the corridor. She was told that in a few hours she might see him. But she wasn't, as a matter of fact, very eager to see him. The knowledge that he was to live, the lifting of the weight of dread, was enough. The maternal strain did not mingle with her love for him; she saw no possible reward, no increased sense of possession, in his illness. On the contrary, she wanted him to stride back in one day from death to his old powerful, dominating self.

She grew to hate the hospital routine, the fixed hours, the regulated food. "These rules, these hovering women," she exclaimed, "these trays - they make me think of the nursery." But what she really hated was Vincent's submission to it all. In her heart she would have been glad to see him breaking the rules, defying the doctors, and bullying his nurses.

Before long a strong, silent antagonism grew up between her and the bright-eyed, cheerful nurse, Miss Gregory. It irritated Adelaide to gain access to her husband through other people's consent; it irritated her to see the girl's understanding of the case, and her competent arrangements for her patient's comfort. If Vincent had showed any disposition to revolt, Adelaide would have pleaded with him to submit; but as it was, she watched his docility with a scornful eye.

"That girl rules you with a rod of iron," she said one day. But even then Vincent did not rouse himself.

"She knows her business," he said admiringly.

To any other invalid Adelaide could have been a soothing visitor, could have adapted the quick turns of her mind to the relaxed attention of the sick; but, honestly enough, there seemed to her an impertinence, almost an insult, in treating Vincent in such a way. The result was that her visits were exhausting, and she knew it. And yet, she said to herself , he was ill, not insane; how could she conceal from him the happenings of every day? Vincent would be the last person to be grateful to her for that.

She saw him one day grow pale; his eyes began to close. She had made up her mind to leave him when Miss Gregory came in, and with a quicker eye and a more active habit of mind, said at once:

"I think Mr. Farron has had enough excitement for one day."

Adelaide smiled up at the girl almost insolently.

"Is a visit from a wife an excitement?" she asked. Miss Gregory was perfectly grave.

"The greatest," she said.

Adelaide yielded to her own irritation.

"Well," she said, "I shan't stay much longer."

"It would be better if you went now, I think,

Mrs. Farron."

Adelaide looked at Vincent. It was silly of him, she thought, to pretend he didn't hear. She bent over him.

"Your nurse is driving me away from you, dearest," she murmured.

He opened his eyes and took her hand.

"Come back to-morrow early - as early as you can," he said.

She never remembered his siding against her before, and she swept out into the hallway, saying to herself that it was childish to be annoyed at the whims of an invalid.

Miss Gregory had followed her.

"Mrs. Farron," she said, "do you mind my suggesting that for the present it would be better not to talk to Mr. Farron about anything that might worry him, even trifles?"

Adelaide laughed.

"You know very little of Mr. Farron," she said, "if you think he worries over trifles."

"Any one worries over trifles when he is in a nervous state."

Adelaide passed by without answering, passed by as if she had not heard. The suggestion of Vincent nervously worrying over trifles was one of the most repellent pictures that had ever been presented to her imagination.

CHAPTER IX

The firm for which Wayne worked was young and small - Benson & Honaton. They made a specialty of circularization in connection with the bond issues in which they were interested, and Wayne had charge of their "literature," as they described it. He often felt, after he had finished a report, that his work deserved the title. A certain number of people in Wall Street disapproved of the firm's methods. Sometimes Pete thought this was because, for a young firm, they had succeeded too quickly to please the more deliberate; but sometimes in darker moments he thought there might be some justice in the idea.

During the weeks that Farron was in the hospital Pete, despite his constant availability to Mathilde, had been at work on his report on a coal property in Pennsylvania. He was extremely pleased with the thoroughness with which he had done the job. His report was not favorable. The day after it was finished, a little after three, he received word that the firm wanted to see him. He was always annoyed with himself that these messages caused his heart to beat a trifle faster. He couldn't help associating them with former hours with his head-master or in the dean's office. Only he had respected his head-master and even the dean, whereas he was not at all sure he respected Mr. Benson and he was quite sure he did not respect Mr. Honaton.

Alice Duer Miller

He rose slowly from his desk, exchanging with the office boy who brought the message a long, severe look, under which something very comic lurked, though neither knew what.

"And don't miss J.B.'s socks," said the boy.

Mr. Honaton - J.B. - was considered in his office a very beautiful dresser, as indeed in some ways he was. He was a tall young man, built like a greyhound, with a small, pointed head, a long waist, and a very long throat, from which, however, the strongest, loudest voice could issue when he so desired. This was his priceless asset. He was the board member, and generally admitted to be an excellent broker. It always seemed to Pete that he was a broker exactly as a beaver is a dam-builder, because nature had adapted him to that task. But outside of this one instinctive capacity he had no sense whatsoever. He rarely appeared in the office. He was met at the Broad Street entrance of the exchange at one minute to ten by a boy with the morning's orders, and sometimes he came in for a few minutes after the closing; but usually by three-fifteen he had disappeared from financial circles, and was understood to be relaxing in the higher social spheres to which he belonged. So when Pete, entering Mr. Benson's private office, saw Honaton leaning against the window-frame, with his hat-brim held against his thigh exactly like a fashion-plate, he knew that something of importance must be pending.

Benson, the senior member, was a very different person. He looked like a fat, white, pugnacious cat. His hair, which had turned white early, had a tendency to grow in a bang; his arms were short - so short that when he put his hands on the arms of his swing-chair he hardly bent his elbows. He had them there now as Pete entered, and was swinging through short arcs in rather a nervous rhythm. He was of Irish parentage, and was understood to have political influence.

"Wayne," said Benson, "how would you like to go to China?"

And Honaton repeated portentously, "China," as if Benson might have made a mistake in the name of the country if he had not been at his elbow to correct him.

Wayne laughed.

"Well," he said, "I have nothing against China."

Benson outlined the situation quickly. The firm had acquired property in China not entirely through their own choice, and they wanted a thorough, clear report on it; they knew of no one - *no one*, Benson emphasized - who could do that as impartially and as well as Wayne. They would pay him a good sum and his expenses. It would take him a year, perhaps a year and a half. They named the figure. It was one that made marriage possible. They talked of the situation and the property and the demand for copper until Honaton began to look at his watch, a flat platinum watch, perfectly plain, you might have thought, until you caught a glimpse of a narrow line of brilliants along its almost imperceptible rim. His usual working day was over in half an hour.

"And when I come back, Mr. Benson?" said Wayne.

"Your place will be open for you here."

There was a pause.

"Well, what do you say?" said Honaton.

"I feel very grateful for the offer," said Pete, "but of course I can't give you an answer now."

"Why not, why not?" returned Honaton, who felt that he had given up half an hour for nothing if the thing couldn't be settled on the spot; and even Benson, Wayne noticed, began to glower.

"You could probably give us as good an answer to-day as to-morrow," he said.

Nothing roused Pete's spirit like feeling a tremor in his own soul, and so he now answered with great firmness:

"I cannot give you an answer to-day *or* to-morrow."

"It's all off, then, all off," said Honaton, moving to the door.

"When do the Chinese boats sail, Mr. Honaton?" said Pete, with the innocence of manner that an employee should use when putting his superior in a hole.

"I don't see what difference that makes to you, Wayne, if you're not taking them," said Honaton, as if he were triumphantly concealing the fact that he didn't know.

"Don't feel you have to wait, Jack, if you're in a hurry," said his partner, and when the other had slid out of the office Benson turned to Wayne and went on: "You wouldn't have to go until a week from Saturday. You would have to get off then, and we should have to know in time to find some one else in case you don't care for it."

Pete asked for three days, and presently left the office.

He had a friend, one of his mother's reformed drunkards, who as janitor lived on the top floor of a tall building. He and his wife offered Wayne the hospitality of their balcony, and now and then, in moments like this, he availed himself of it. Not, indeed, that there had ever been a moment quite like this; for he knew that he was facing the most important decision he had ever been forced to make.

In the elevator he met the janitor's cat Susan going home after an afternoon visit to the restaurant on the sixteenth floor. The elevator boy loved to tell how she never made a mistake in the floor.

"Do you think she'd get off at the fifteenth or the seventeenth? Not she. Sometimes she puts her nose out and smells at the other floors, but she won't get off until I stop at the right one. Sometimes she has to ride up and down three or four times before any one wants the sixteenth. Eh, Susan?" he added in caressing tones; but Susan was watching the floors flash past and paid no attention until, arrived at the top, she and Pete stepped off together.

It was a cool, clear day, for the wind was from the north, but on the southern balcony the sun was warm. Pete sat down in the kitchen-chair set for him, tilted back, and looked out over the Statue of Liberty, which stood like a stunted baby, to the blue Narrows. He saw one thing clearly, and that was that he would not go if Mathilde would not go with him.

He envied people who could make up their minds by thinking. At least sometimes he envied them and sometimes he thought they lied. He could only think *about* a subject and wait for the unknown gods to bring him a decision. And this is what he now did, with his eyes fixed on the towers and tanks and tenements, on the pale winter sky, and, when he got up and leaned his elbows on the parapet, on the crowds that looked like a flood of purple insects in the streets.

He thought of Mathilde's youth and his own untried capacities for success, of poverty and children, of the probable opposition of Mathilde's family and of a strange, sinister, disintegrating power he felt or suspected in Mrs. Farron. He felt that it was a terrible risk to ask a young girl to take and that it was almost an insult to be afraid to ask her to take it. That was what his mother had always said about these cherished, protected creatures: they were not prepared to meet any strain in life. He knew he would not have hesitated to ask a girl differently brought up. Ought he to ask Mathilde or ought he not even to hesitate about asking her? In his own future he had confidence. He had an unusual power of getting his facts together so that they meant something. In a small way his work was recognized. A report of his had some weight. He felt certain that if on his return he wanted another position he could get it unless he made a terrible fiasco in China. Should he consult any one? He knew beforehand what they would all think about it. Mr. Lanley would think that it was sheer impertinence to want to marry his granddaughter on less than fifteen thousand dollars a year; Mrs. Farron would think that there were lots of equally agreeable young men in the world who would not take a girl to China; and his mother, whom he could not help considering the wisest of the three, would think that Mathilde lacked discipline and strength of will for such an adventure. And on this he found he made up his mind. "After all," he said to himself as he put the chair back against the wall, "everything else would be failure, and this may be success."

It was the afternoon that Farron was brought back from the hospital, and he and Mathilde were sure of having the drawing-room to themselves. He told her the situation slowly and with a great deal of detail, chronologically, introducing the Chinese trip at the very end. But she did not at once understand.

"O Pete, you would not go away from me!" she said. "I could not face that."

"Couldn't you? Remember that everything you say is going to be used against you."

"Would you be willing to go, Pete?"

"Only if you will go with me."

"Oh!" she clasped her hands to her breast, shrinking back to look at him. So that was what he had meant, this stranger whom she had known for such a short time. As she looked she half expected that he would smile, and say it was all a joke; but his eyes were steadily and seriously fixed on hers. It was very queer, she thought. Their meeting, their first kiss, their engagement, had all seemed so inevitable, so natural, there had not been a hint of doubt or decision about it; but now all of a sudden she found herself faced by a situation in which it was impossible to say yes or no.

"It would be wonderful, of course," she said, after a minute, but her tone showed she was not considering it as a possibility.

Wayne's heart sank; he saw that he had thought it possible that he would not allow her to go, but that he had never seriously faced the chance of her refusing.

"Mathilde," he said, "it's far and sudden, and we shall be poor, and I can't promise that I shall succeed more than other fellows; and yet against all that -"

She looked at him.

"You don't think I care for those things? I don't care if you succeed or fail, or live all your life in Siam."

"What is it, then?"

"Pete, it's my mother. She would never consent."

Wayne was aware of this, but, then, as he pointed out to Mathilde with great care, Mrs. Farron could not bear for her daughter the pain of separation.

"Separation!" cried the girl, "But you just said you would not go if I did not."

"If you put your mother before me, mayn't I put my profession before you?"

"My dear, don't speak in that tone."

"Why, Mathilde," he said, and he sprang up and stood looking down at her from a little distance, "this is the real test. We have thought we loved each other -"

"Thought!" she interrupted.

"But to get engaged with no immediate prospect of marriage, with all our families and friends grouped about, that doesn't mean such a lot, does it?"

"It does to me," she answered almost proudly.

"Now, one of us has to sacrifice something. I want to go on this expedition. I want to succeed. That may be egotism or legitimate ambition. I don't know, but I want to go. I think I mean to go. Ought I to give it up because you are afraid of your mother?"

"It's love, not fear, Pete."

"You love me, too, you say."

"I feel an obligation to her."

"And, good Heavens! do you feel none to me?"

"No, no. I love you too much to feel an obligation to you."

"But you love your mother *and* feel an obligation to her. Why, Mathilde, that feeling of obligation *is* love - love in its most serious form. That's what you don't feel for me. That's why you won't go."

"I haven't said I wouldn't go."

"You never even thought of going."

"I have, I do. But how can I help hesitating? You must know I want to go."

"I see very little sign of it," he murmured. The interview had not gone as he intended. He had not meant, he never imagined, that he would attempt to urge and coerce her; but her very detachment seemed to set a fire burning within him.

"I think," he said with an effort to sound friendly, "that I had better go and let you think this over by yourself."

He was actually moving to the door when she sprang up and put her arms about him.

"Weren't you even going to kiss me, Pete?"

He stooped, and touched her cheek with his lips.

"Do you call that a kiss?"

"O Mathilde, do you think any kiss will change the facts?" he answered, and was gone.

As soon as he had left her the desire for tears left her, too. She felt calm and more herself, more an isolated, independent human being than ever before in her life. She thought of all the things she ought to have said to Pete. The reason why she felt no obligation to him was that she was one with him. She was prepared to sacrifice him exactly as she was, or ought to be, willing to sacrifice herself; whereas her mother - it seemed as if her mother's power surrounded her in every direction, as solid as the ancients believed the dome of heaven.

Pringle appeared in the doorway in his eternal hunt for the tea-things.

"May I take the tray, miss?" he said.

She nodded, hardly glancing at the untouched tea-table. Pringle, as he bent over it, observed that it was nice to have Mr. Farron back. Mathilde remembered that she, too, had once been interested in her stepfather's return.

"Where's my mother, Pringle?"

"Mrs. Farron's in her room, I think, miss, and Mr. Lanley's with her."

Lanley had stopped as usual to ask after his son-in-law. He found his daughter writing letters in her room. He thought her looking cross, but in deference to her recent anxieties he called it, even in his own mind, overstrained.

"Vincent is doing very well, I believe," she answered in response to his question. "He ought to be. He is in charge of two lovely young creatures hardly Mathilde's age who have already taken complete control of the household."

"You've seen him, of course."

"For a few minutes; they allow me a few minutes. They communicate by secret signals when they think I have stayed long enough."

Mr. Lanley never knew how to treat this mood of his daughter's, which seemed to him as unreasonable as if it were emotional, and yet as cold as if it were logic itself. He changed the subject and said boldly:

Alice Duer Miller

"Mrs. Baxter is coming to-morrow."

Adelaide's eyes faintly flashed.

"Oh, wouldn't you know it!" she murmured. "Just at the most inconvenient time - inconvenient for me, I mean. Really, lovers are the only people you can depend on. I wish I had a lover."

"Adelaide," said her father with some sternness, "even in fun you should not say such a thing. If Mathilde heard you -"

"Mathilde is the person who made me see it. Her boy is here all the time, trying to think of something to please her. And who have I? Vincent has his nurses; and you have your old upholstered lady. I can't help wishing I had a lover. They are the only people who, as the Wayne boy would say, 'stick around.' But don't worry, Papa, I have a loyal nature." She was interrupted by a knock at the door, and a nurse - the same who had been too encouraging to please her at the hospital - put in her head and said brightly:

"You may see Mr. Farron now, Mrs. Farron."

Adelaide turned to her father and made a little bow.

"See how I am favored," she said, and left him.

Nothing of this mood was apparent when she entered her husband's room, though she noticed that the arrangement of the furniture had been changed, and, what she disliked even more, that they had brushed his hair in a new way. This, with his pallor and thinness, made him look strange to her. She bent over, and laid her cheek to his almost motionless lips.

"Well, dear," she said, "have you seen the church-warden part they have given your hair?"

He shook his head impatiently, and she saw, she had made the mistake of trying to give the tone to an interview in which she was not the leading character.

"Who has the room above mine, Adelaide?" he asked.

"My maid."

"Ask her not to practice the fox-trot, will you?"

"O Vincent, she is never there."

"My mistake," he answered, and shut his eyes.

She repented at once.

"Of course I'll tell her. I'm sorry that you were disturbed." But she was thinking only of his tone. He was not an irritable man, and he had never used such a tone to her before. All pleasure in the interview was over. She was actually glad when one of the nurses came in and began to move about the room in a manner that suggested dismissal.

"Of course I'm not angry," she said to herself. "He's so weak one must humor him like a child."

She derived some satisfaction, however, from the idea of sending for her maid Lucie and making her uncom-fortable; but on her way she met Mathilde in the hall.

"May I speak to you, Mama?" she said.

Mrs. Farron laughed.

"May you speak to me?" she said. "Why, yes; you may have the unusual privilege. What is it?"

Mathilde followed her mother into the bedroom and shut the door.

"Pete has just been here. He has been offered a position in China."

"In China?" said Mrs. Farron. This was the first piece of luck that had come to her in a long time, but she did not betray the least pleasure. "I hope it is a good one."

"Yes, he thinks it good. He sails in two weeks."

"In two weeks?" And this time she could not prevent her eye lighting a little. She thought how nicely that small complication had settled itself, and how clever she had been to have the mother to dinner and behave as if she were friendly. She did not notice that her daughter was trembling; she couldn't, of course, be expected to know that the girl's hands were like ice, and that she had waited several seconds to steady her voice sufficiently to pronounce the fatal sentence:

"He wants me to go with him, Mama."

She watched her mother in an agony for the effect of these words. Mrs. Farron had suddenly detected a new burn in the hearth-rug. She bent over it.

"This wood does snap so!" she murmured.

The rug was a beautiful old Persian carpet of roses and urns.

"Did you understand what I said, Mama?"

"Yes, dear; that Mr. Wayne was going to China in two weeks and wanted you to go, too. Was it just a *politesse*, or does he actually imagine that you could?"

"He thinks I can."

Mrs. Farron laughed good-temperedly.

"Did you go and see about having your pink silk shortened?" she said.

Mathilde stared at her mother, and in the momentary silence Lucie came in and asked what madame wanted for the evening, and Adelaide in her fluent French began explaining that what she really desired most was that Lucie should not make so much noise in her room that monsieur could not sleep. In the midst of it she stopped and turned to her daughter.

"Won't you be late for dinner, darling?" she said.

Mathilde thought it very possible, and went away to get dressed. She went into her own room and shut the door sharply behind her.

All the time she was dressing she tried to rehearse her case - that it was her life, her love, her chance; but all the time she had a sickening sense that a lifted eyebrow of her mother's would make it sound childish and absurd even in her own ears. She had counted on a long evening, but when she went down-stairs she

Alice Duer Miller

found three or four friends of her mother's were to dine and go to the theater. The dinner was amusing, the talk, though avowedly hampered by the presence of Mathilde, was witty and unexpected enough; but Mathilde was not amused by it, for she particularly dreaded her mother in such a mood of ruthless gaiety. At the theater they were extremely critical, and though they missed almost the whole first act, appeared, in the entr'acte, to feel no hesitation in condemning it. They spoke of French and Italian actors by name, laughed heartily over the playwright's conception of social usages, and made Mathilde feel as if her own unacknowledged enjoyment of the play was the guiltiest of secrets.

As they drove home, she was again alone with her mother, and she said at once the sentence she had determined on:

"I don't think you understood, Mama, how seriously I meant what I said this afternoon."

Mrs. Farron was bending her long-waisted figure forward to get a good look at a picture which, small, lonely, and brightly lighted, hung in a picture-dealer's window. It was a picture of an empty room. Hot summer sunlight filtered through the lowered Venetian blinds, and fell in bands on the golden wood of the floor. Outside the air was burned and dusty, but inside the room all was clear, cool, and pure.

"How perfect his things are," murmured Mrs. Farron to herself, and then added to her daughter: "Yes, my dear, I did take in what you said. You really think you are in love with this Wayne boy, don't you? It's immensely to your credit, darling," she went on, her tone taking on a flattering sweetness, "to care so much about any one who has such funny, stubby little hands - most unattractive hands," she added almost dreamily.

There was a long pause during which an extraordinary thing happened to Mathilde. She found that it didn't make the very slightest difference to her what her mother thought of Pete or his hands, that it would never make any difference to her again. It was as if her will had suddenly been born, and the first act of that will was to decide to go with the man she loved. How could she have doubted for an instant? It was so simple, and no opposition would or could mean anything to her. She was not in the least angry; on the contrary, she felt extremely pitiful, as if she were saying good-by to some one who did not know she was going away, as if in a sense she had now parted from her mother forever. Tears came into her eyes.

"Ah, Mama!" she said like a sigh.

Mrs. Farron felt she had been cruel, but without regretting it; for that, she thought, was often a parent's duty.

"I don't want to hurt your feelings, Mathilde. The boy is a nice enough little person, but really I could not let you set off for China at a minute's notice with any broker's clerk who happened to fall in love with your golden hair. When you have a little more experience you will discriminate between the men you like to have love you and the men there is the smallest chance of your loving. I assure you, if little Wayne were not in love with you, you would think him a perfectly commonplace boy. If one of your friends were engaged to him, you would be the first to say that you wondered what it was she saw in him. That isn't the way one wants people to feel about one's husband, is it? And as to going to China with him, you know that's impossible, don't you?"

"It would be impossible to let him go without me."

"Really, Mathilde!" said Mrs. Farron, gently, as if she, so willing to play fair, were being put off with fantasies. "I don't understand you," she added.

"No, Mama; you don't."

The motor stopped at the door, and they went in silence to Mrs. Farron's room, where for a bitter hour they talked, neither yielding an inch. At last Adelaide sent the girl to bed. Mathilde was aware of profound physical exhaustion, and yet underneath there was a high knowledge of something unbreakable within her.

Left alone, Adelaide turned instinctively toward her husband's door. There were her strength and vision. Then she remembered, and drew back; but presently, hearing a stir there, she knocked very softly. A nurse appeared on the instant.

"Oh, *please*, Mrs. Farron! Mr. Farron has just got to sleep."

Adelaide stood alone in the middle of the floor. Once again, she thought, in a crisis of her life she had no one to depend on but herself. She lifted her shoulders. No one was to blame, but there the fact was. They urged you to cling and be guided, but when the pinch came, you had to act for yourself. She had learned her lesson now. Henceforward she took her own life over into her own hands.

She reviewed her past dependences. Her youth, with its dependence on her father, particularly in matters of dress. She recalled her early photographs with a shudder. Had she really dressed so badly or was it only the change of fashion? And then her dependence on Joe Severance. What could be more ridiculous than for a woman of her intelligence to allow herself to be guided in everything by a man like Joe, who had nothing himself but a certain shrewd masculinity? And now Vincent. She was still under the spell of his superiority, but perhaps she would come to judge him too. She had learned much from him. Perhaps she had learned all he had to teach her. Her face looked as if it were carved out of some smooth white stone.

CHAPTER X

After she had gone up-stairs, Mathilde went down again to telephone Pete that she had made her decision. She went boldly snapping electric switches, for her going was a sort of assertion of her right to independent action. She would have hesitated even less if she had known how welcome her news was, how he had suffered since their parting.

On going home from his interview with her, he found his mother dressing to dine with Mr. Lanley, a party arranged before the unexpected arrival of Mrs. Baxter. The only part of dressing that delayed Mrs. Wayne was her hair, which was so long that the brushing of it took time. In this process she was engaged when her son, in response to her answer, came into her room.

"How is Mr. Farron?" she asked at once, and he, rather touched at the genuineness of her interest, answered her in detail before her next exclamation betrayed that it was entirely for the employer of Marty Burke that she was solicitous. "Isn't it too bad he was taken ill just now?" she said.

The bitterness and doubt from which Wayne was suffering were not emotions that disposed him to confidence. He did not want to tell his mother what he was going through, for the obvious and perhaps unworthy reason that it was just what she would have expected him to go through. At the same time a real deceit was involved in concealing it, and so, tipping his chair back against her wall, he said:

"The firm has asked me to go to China for them."

His mother turned, her whole face lit up with interest.

"To China! How interesting!" she said. "China is a wonderful country. How I should like to go to China!"

"Come along. I don't start for two weeks."

She shook her head.

"No, if you go, I'll make a trip to that hypnotic clinic of Dr. Platerbridge's; and if I can learn the trick, I will open one here."

The idea crossed Wayne's mind that perhaps he had not the power of inspiring affection.

"You don't miss people a bit, do you, Mother?" he said.

"Yes, Pete, I do; only there is so much to be done. What does Mathilde say to you going off like this? How long will you be gone?"

"More than a year."

"Pete, how awful for her!"

"There is nothing to prevent her going with me."

"You couldn't take that child to China."

"You may be glad to know that she is cordially of your opinion."

The feeling behind his tone at last attracted his mother's full attention.

"But, my dear boy," she said gently, "she has never been anywhere in her life without a maid. She probably doesn't know how to do her hair or mend her clothes or anything practical."

"Mother dear, you are not so awfully practical yourself," he answered; "but you would have gone."

Mrs. Wayne looked impish.

"I always loved that sort of thing," she said; and then, becoming more maternal, she added, "and that doesn't mean it would be sensible because I'd do it."

"Well," - Wayne stood up preparatory to leaving the room, - "I mean to take her if she'll go."

His mother, who had now finished winding her braid very neatly around her head, sank into a chair.

"Oh, dear!" she said, "I almost wish I weren't dining with Mr. Lanley. He'll think it's all my fault."

"I doubt if he knows about it."

Mrs. Wayne's eyes twinkled.

"May I tell him? I should like to see his face."

"Tell him I am going, if you like. Don't say I want to

take her with me."

Her face fell.

"That wouldn't be much fun," she answered, "because I suppose the truth is they won't be sorry to have you out of the way."

"I suppose not," he said, and shut the door behind him. He could not truthfully say that his mother had been much of a comfort. He had suddenly thought that he would go down to the first floor and get Lily Parret to go to the theater with him. He and she had the warm friendship for each other of two handsome, healthy young people of opposite sexes who might have everything to give each other except time. She was perhaps ten years older than he, extremely handsome, with dimples and dark red hair and blue eyes. She had a large practice among the poor, and might have made a conspicuous success of her profession if it had not been for her intense and too widely diffused interest. She wanted to strike a blow at every abuse that came to her attention, and as, in the course of her work, a great many turned up, she was always striking blows and never following them up. She went through life in a series of springs, each one in a different direction; but the motion of her attack was as splendid as that of a tiger. Often she was successful, and always she enjoyed herself.

When she answered Pete's ring, and he looked up at her magnificent height, her dimples appeared in welcome. She really was glad to see him.

"Come out and dine with me, Lily, and go to the theater."

"Come to a meeting at Cooper Union on capital punishment. I'm going to speak, and I'm going to be very good."

"No, Lily; I want to explain to you what a pitiable sex you belong to. You have no character, no will -"

She shook her head, laughing.

"You are a personal lot, you young men," she said. "You change your mind about women every day, according to how one of them treats you."

"They don't amount to a row of pins, Lily."

"Certainly some men select that kind, Pete."

"O Lily," he answered, "don't talk to me like that! I want some one to tell me I'm perfect, and, strangely enough, no one will."

"I will," she answered, with beaming good nature, "and I pretty near think so, too. But I can't dine with you, Pete. Wouldn't you like to go to my meeting?"

"I should perfectly hate to," he answered, and went off crossly, to dine at his college's local club. Here he found an old friend, who most fortunately said something derogatory of the firm of Benson & Honaton. The opinion coincided with certain phases of Wayne's own views, but he contradicted it, held it up to ridicule, and ended by quoting incidents in the history of his friend's own firm which, as he said, were probably among the crookedest things that had ever been put over in Wall Street. Lily would not have distracted his mind more completely. He felt almost cheerful when he went home about ten o'clock. His mother was still out, and there was no letter from Mathilde. He had been counting on finding one.

Before long his mother came in. She was looking very fine. She had on a new gray dress that she had had made for her by a fallen woman from an asylum, but which had turned out better than such ventures of Mrs. Wayne's usually did.

She had supposed she and Mr. Lanley were to dine alone, an idea which had not struck her as revolutionary. Accustomed to strange meals in strange company - a bowl of milk with a prison chaplain at a dairy lunch-room, or even, on one occasion, a supper in an Owl Lunch Wagon with a wavering drunkard, - she had thought that a quiet, perfect dinner with Mr. Lanley sounded pleasant enough. But she was not sorry to find it had been enlarged. She liked to meet new people. She was extremely optimistic, and always hoped that they would prove either spiritually rewarding, or practically useful to some of her projects. When she saw Mrs. Baxter, with her jetty hair, jeweled collar, and eyes a trifle too saurian for perfect beauty, she at once saw a subscription to the working-girl's club. The fourth person Mr. Wilsey, Lanley's lawyer, she knew well by reputation. She wondered if she could make him see that his position on the eight-hour law was absolutely anti-social.

Mr. Lanley enjoyed a small triumph when she entered. He had been so discreet in his description of her to Mrs. Baxter, he had been so careful not to hint that she was an illuminating personality who had suddenly come into his life, that he knew he had left his old friend with the general impression that Mrs. Wayne was merely the mother of an undesirable suitor of Mathilde's who spent most of her life in the company of drunkards. So when she came in, a little late as usual, in her long, soft, gray dress, with a pink rose at her girdle, looking far more feminine than Mrs. Baxter, about whom Adelaide's offensive adjective "uphol-stered" still clung, he felt the full effect of her appearance. He even enjoyed the obviously suspicious glance which Mrs. Baxter immediately afterward turned upon him.

At dinner things began well. They talked about people and events of which Mrs. Wayne knew nothing, but her interest and good temper made her not an outsider, but an audience. Anecdotes which even Mr. Lanley might have felt were trivial gossip became, through her attention to them, incidents of the highest human interest. Such an uncritical interest was perhaps too stimulating.

He expected nothing dangerous when, during the game course, Mrs. Baxter turned to him and asked how Mathilde had enjoyed what she referred to as "her first winter."

Mr. Lanley liked to talk about Mathilde. He described, with a little natural exaggeration, how much she had enjoyed herself and how popular she had been.

"I hope she hasn't been bitten by any of those modern notions," said Mrs. Baxter.

Mr. Wilsey broke in.

"Oh, these modern, restless young women!" he said. "They don't seem able to find their natural contentment in their own homes. My daughter came to me the other day with a wonderful scheme of working all day long with charity organizations. I said to her, 'My dear, charity begins at home.' My wife, Mrs. Baxter, is an old-fashioned housekeeper. She gives out all supplies used in my house; she knows where the servants are at every minute of the day, and we have nine. She -"

"Oh, how is dear Mrs. Wilsey?" said Mrs. Baxter, perhaps not eager for the full list of her activities.

"Well, at present she is in a sanatorium," replied her husband, "from overwork, just plain overwork."

Mr. Lanley, catching Mrs. Wayne's twinkling eye, could only pray that she would not point out that a sojourn in a sanatorium was not complete contentment in the home; but before she had a chance, Mrs. Baxter had gone on.

"That's so like the modern girl - anything but her obvious duty. She'll help any one but her mother and work anywhere but in the home. We've had a very painful case at home lately. One of our most charming young girls has suddenly developed an absolutely morbid curiosity about the things that take place in the women's courts. Why, as her poor father said to me, 'Mrs. Baxter, old as I am, I hear things in those courts so shocking I have hard work forgetting them; and yet Imogen wants me to let her go into those courts day after day - '"

"Oh, that's abnormal, almost perverted," said Mr. Wilsey, judicially. "The women's courts are places where no -" he hesitated a bare instant, and Mrs. Wayne asked:

Alice Duer Miller

"No woman should go?"

"No girl should go."

"Yet many of the girls who come there are under sixteen."

Mr. Wilsey hid a slight annoyance under a manner peculiarly bland.

"Ah, dear lady," he said, "you must forgive my saying that that remark is a trifle irrelevant."

"Is it?" she asked, meaning him to answer her; but he only looked benevolently at her, and turned to listen to Mrs. Baxter, who was saying:

"Yes, everywhere we look nowadays we see women rushing into things they don't understand, and of course we all know what women are -"

"What are they?" asked Mrs. Wayne, and Lanley's heart sank.

"Oh, emotional and inaccurate and untrustworthy and spiteful."

"Mrs. Baxter, I'm sure you're not like that."

"My dear Madam!" exclaimed Wilsey.

"But isn't that logical?" Mrs. Wayne pursued. "If all women are so, and she's a woman?"

" Ah, logic, dear lady," said Wilsey, holding up a finger - "logic, you know, has never been the specialty of your sex."

"Of course it's logic," said Lanley, crossly. "If you say all Americans are liars, Wilsey, and you're an American, the logical inference is that you think yourself a liar. But Mrs. Baxter doesn't mean that she thinks all women are inferior -"

"I must say I prefer men," she answered almost coquettishly.

"If all women were like you, Mrs. Baxter, I'd believe in giving them the vote," said Wilsey.

"Please don't," she answered. "I don't want it."

"Ah, the clever ones don't."

"I never pretended to be clever."

"Perhaps not; but I'd trust your intuition where I would pay no attention to a clever person."

Lanley laughed.

"I think you'd better express that a little differently, Wilsey," he said; but his legal adviser did not notice him.

"My daughter came to me the other day," he went on to Mrs. Baxter, "and said, 'Father, don't you think women ought to have the vote some day?' and I said, 'Yes, my dear, just as soon as men have the babies.'"

"There's no answer to that," said Mrs. Baxter.

"I fancy not," said Wilsey. "I think I put the essence of it in that sentence."

"If ever women get into power in this country, I shall live abroad."

"O Mrs. Baxter," said Mrs. Wayne, "really you don't understand women -"

"I don't? Why, Mrs. Wayne, I am a woman."

"All human beings are spiteful and inaccurate and all those things you said; but that isn't *all* they are. The women I see, the wives of my poor drunkards are so wonderful, so patient. They are mothers and wage-earners and sick nurses, too; they're not the sort of women you describe. Perhaps," she added, with one of her fatal impulses toward concession, "perhaps your friends are untrustworthy and spiteful, as you say -"

Mrs. Baxter drew herself up. "My friends, Mrs. Wayne," she said - "my friends, I think, will compare favorably even with the wives of your drunkards."

Mr. Lanley rose to his feet.

"Shall we go up-stairs?" he said. Mr. Wilsey offered Mrs. Baxter his arm. "An admirable answer that of yours," he murmured as he led her from the room, "admirable snub to her perfectly unwarranted attack on you and your friends."

"Of course you realize that she doesn't know any of the people I know," said Mrs. Baxter. "Why should she begin to abuse them?"

Mr. Wilsey laughed, and shook his finger.

"Just because she doesn't know them. That, I'm afraid, is the rub. That's what I usually find lies behind the socialism of socialists - the sense of being excluded. This poor lady has evidently very little *usage du monde*. It is her pitiful little protest, dear Madam, against your charm, your background, your grand manner."

They sank upon an ample sofa near the fire, and though the other end of the large room was chilly, Lanley and Mrs. Wayne moved thither with a common impulse.

Mrs. Wayne turned almost tearfully to Lanley.

"I'm so sorry I've spoiled your party," she said.

"You've done much worse than that," he returned gravely.

"O Mr. Lanley," she wailed, "what have I done?"

"You've spoiled a friendship."

"Between you and me?"

He shook his head.

"Between them and me. I never heard people talk such nonsense, and yet I've been hearing people talk like that all my life, and have never taken it in. Mrs. Wayne, I want you to tell me something frankly -"

"Oh, I'm so terrible when I'm frank," she said.

"Do I talk like that?"

She looked at him and looked away again.

"Good God! you think I do!"

"No, you don't talk like that often, but I think you feel that way a good deal."

"I don't want to," he answered. "I'm sixty-four, but I don't ever want to talk like Wilsey. Won't you stop me whenever I do?"

Mrs. Wayne sighed.

"It will make you angry."

"And if it does?"

"I hate to make people angry. I was distressed that evening on the pier."

He looked up, startled.

"I suppose I talked like Wilsey that night?"

"You said you might be old-fashioned but -"

"Don't, please, tell me what I said, Mrs. Wayne." He went on more seriously: "I've got to an age when I can't expect great happiness from life - just a continuance of fairly satisfactory outside conditions; but since I've known you, I've felt a lightening, a brightening, an intensifying of my own inner life that I believe comes as near happiness as anything I've ever felt, and I don't want to lose it on account of a reactionary old couple like that on the sofa over there."

He dreaded being left alone with the reactionary old couple when presently Mrs. Wayne, very well pleased with her evening, took her departure. He assisted her into her taxi, and as he came upstairs with a buoyant step, he wished it were not ridiculous at his age to feel so light-hearted.

He saw that his absence had given his guests an instant of freer criticism, for they were tucking away smiles as he entered.

"A very unusual type, is she not, our friend, Mrs. Wayne?" said Wilsey.

"A little bit of a reformer, I'm afraid," said Mrs. Baxter.

"Don't be too hard on her," answered Lanley.

"Oh, very charming, very charming," put in Wilsey, feeling, perhaps, that Mrs. Baxter had been severe; "but the poor lady's mind is evidently seething with a good many undigested ideas."

"You should have pointed out the flaws in her reasoning, Wilsey," said his host.

"Argue with a woman, Lanley!" Mr. Wilsey held up his hand in protest. "No, no, I never argue with a woman. They take it so personally."

"I think we had an example of that this evening," said Mrs. Baxter.

"Yes, indeed," the lawyer went on. "See how the dear lady missed the point, and became so illogical and excited under our little discussion."

"Funny," said Lanley. "I got just the opposite impression."

"Opposite?"

"I thought it was you who missed the point, Wilsey."

He saw how deeply he had betrayed himself as the others exchanged a startled glance. It was Mrs. Baxter who thought of the correct reply.

"*Were* there any points?" she asked.

Wilsey shook his finger.

"Ah, don't be cruel!" he said, and held out his hand to say good night; but Lanley was smoking, with his head tilted up and his eyes on the ceiling. What he was thinking was, "It isn't good for an old man to get as angry as I am."

"Good night, Lanley; a delightful evening."

Mr. Lanley's chin came down.

"Oh, good night, Wilsey; glad you found it so."

When he was gone, Mrs. Baxter observed that he was a most agreeable companion.

"So witty, so amiable, and, for a leader at the bar, he has an extraordinarily light touch."

Mr. Lanley had resumed his position on the hearth-rug and his contemplation of the ceiling.

"Wilsey's not a leader at the bar," he said, with open crossness.

He showed no disposition to sit and chat over the events of the evening.

CHAPTER XI

Early the next morning, in Mrs. Baxter's parlance, - that is to say, some little time before the sun had reached the meridian, - she was ringing Adelaide's door-bell, while she minutely observed the curtains, the door-mat, the ivy plants in the vestibule, and the brightness of the brass knobs on the railing. In this she had a double motive: what was evil she would criticize, what was good she would copy.

Adelaide was sitting with her husband when her visitor's name was brought up. Since she had discovered that she was to be nothing but a sort of super-nurse to him, she found herself expert at rendering such service. She had brought in his favorite flowers, chosen a book for his bedside, and now sat gossiping beside him, not bringing him, as she said to herself, any of her real troubles; that would not be good for him. How extraordinarily easy it was to conceal, she thought. She heard her own tones, as gay and intimate as ever, as satisfactory to Vincent; and yet all the time her mind was working apart on her anxieties about Mathilde - anxieties with which, of course, one couldn't bother a poor sick creature. She smoothed his pillow with the utmost tenderness.

"Oh, Pringle," she said, in answer to his announcement that Mrs. Baxter was down-stairs, "you haven't let her in?"

"She's in the drawing-room, Madam." And Pringle added as a clear indication of what he considered her duty, "She came in Mr. Lanley's motor."

"Of course she did. Well, say I'll be down," and as Pringle went away with this encouraging intelligence, Adelaide sank even farther back in her chair and looked at her husband. "What I am called upon to sacrifice to other people's love affairs! The Waynes and Mrs. Baxter - I never have time for my own friends. I don't mind Mrs. Baxter when you're well, and I can have a dinner; I ask all the stupid people together to whom I owe parties, and she is so pleased with them, and thinks they represent the most brilliant New York circle; but to have to go down and actually talk to her, isn't that hard, Vin?"

"Hard on me," said Farron.

"Oh, I shall come back - exhausted."

"By what you have given out?"

"No, but by her intense intimacy. You have no idea how well she knows me. It's Adelaide this and Adelaide that and 'the last time you stayed with me in Baltimore.' You know, Vin, I never stayed with her but once, and that only because she found me in the hotel and kidnapped me. However," - Adelaide stood up with determination, -"one good thing is, I have begun to have an effect on my father. He does not like her any more. He was distinctly bored at the prospect of her visit this time. He did not resent it at all when I called her an upholstered old lady. I really think," she added, with modest justice, "that I am rather good at poisoning people's minds against their undesirable friends." She paused, debating how long it would take her to separate Mathilde from the Wayne boy; and recalling that this was no topic for an invalid, she smiled at him and went down-stairs.

"My dear Adelaide!" said Mrs. Baxter, enveloping her in a powdery caress.

"How wonderfully you're looking, Mrs. Baxter," said Adelaide, choosing her adverb with intention.

"Now tell me, dear," said Mrs. Baxter, with a wave of a gloved hand, "what are those Italian embroideries?"

"Those?" Adelaide lifted her eyebrows. "Ah, you're in fun! A collector like you! Surely you know what those are."

"No," answered Mrs. Baxter, firmly, though she wished she had selected something else to comment on.

"Oh, they are the Villanelli embroideries," said Adelaide, carelessly, very much as if she had said they were the Raphael cartoons, so that Mrs. Baxter was forced to reply in an awestruck tone:

"You don't tell me! Are they, really?"

Adelaide nodded brightly. She had not actually made up the name. It was that of an obscure little palace where she had bought the hangings, and if Mrs. Baxter had had the courage to acknowledge ignorance, Adelaide would have told the truth. As it was, she recognized that by methods such as this she could retain absolute control over people like Mrs. Baxter.

The lady from Baltimore decided on a more general scope.

"Ah, your room!" she said. "Do you know whose it always reminds me of - that lovely salon of Madame de Liantour's?"

"What, of poor little Henrietta's!" cried Adelaide, and she laid her hand appealingly for an instant on Mrs. Baxter's knee. "That's a cruel thing to say. All her good things, you know, were sold years ago. Everything she has is a reproduction. Am I really like her?"

Getting out of this as best she could on a vague statement about atmosphere and sunshine and charm, Mrs. Baxter took refuge in inquiries about Vincent's health, "your charming child," and "your dear father."

"You know more about my dear father than I do," returned Adelaide, sweetly. It was Mrs. Baxter's cue.

"I did not feel last evening that I knew anything about him at all. He is in a new phase, almost a new personality. Tell me, who is this Mrs. Wayne?"

"Mrs. Wayne?" Mrs. Baxter must have felt herself revenged by the complete surprise of Adelaide's tone.

"Yes, she dined at the house last evening. Apparently it was to have been a tete-a-tete dinner, but my arrival changed it to a *partie carree*." She talked on about Wilsey and the conversation of the evening, but it made little difference what she said, for her full idea had reached Adelaide from the start, and had gathered to itself in an instant a hundred confirmatory memories. Like a picture, she saw before her Mrs. Wayne's sitting-room, with the ink-spots on the rug. Who would not wish to exchange that for Mr. Lanley's series of fresh, beautiful rooms? Suddenly she gave her attention back to Mrs. Baxter, who was saying:

"I assure you, when we were alone I was prepared for a formal announcement."

It was not safe to be the bearer of ill tidings to Adelaide.

"An announcement?" she said wonderingly. "Oh, no, Mrs. Baxter, my father will never marry again. There have always been rumors, and you can't imagine how he and I have laughed over them together."

As the indisputable subject of such rumors in past times, Mrs. Baxter fitted a little arrow in her bow.

"In the past," she said, "women of suitable age have not perhaps been willing to consider the question, but this lady seems to me distinctly willing."

"More than willingness on the lady's part has been needed," answered Adelaide, and then Pringle's ample form appeared in the doorway. "There's a man from the office here, Madam, asking to see Mr. Farron."

"Mr. Farron can see no one." A sudden light flashed upon her. "What is his name, Pringle?"

"Burke, Madam."

"Oh, let him come in." Adelaide turned to Mrs. Baxter. "I will show you," she said, "one of the finest sights you ever saw." The next instant Marty was in the room. Not so gorgeous as in his wedding-attire, he was still an exceedingly fine young animal. He was not so magnificently defiant as before, but he scowled at his unaccustomed surroundings under his dark brows.

"It's Mr. Farron I wanted to see," he said, a soft roll to his r's. At Mrs. Wayne's Adelaide had suffered from being out of her own surroundings, but here she was on her own field, and she meant to make Burke feel it. She was leaning with her elbow on the back of the sofa, and now she slipped her bright rings down her slim fingers and shook them back again as she looked up at Burke and spoke to him as she would have done to a servant.

"Mr. Farron cannot see you."

Cleverer people than Burke had struggled vainly against the poison of inferiority which this tone instilled into their minds.

"That's what they keep telling me down-town. I never knew him sick before."

"No?"

"It wouldn't take five minutes."

"Mr. Farron is too weak to see you."

Marty made a strange grating sound in his throat, and Adelaide asked like a queen bending from the throne:

"What seems to be the matter, Burke?"

"Why," - Burke turned upon her the flare of his light, fierce eyes, - "they have it on me on the dock that as soon as he comes back he means to bounce me."

"To bounce you," repeated Adelaide, and she almost smiled as she thought of that poor exhausted figure up-stairs.

"I don't care if he does or not," Marty went on. "I'm not so damned stuck on the job. There's others."

"There are maidens in Scotland more lovely by far," murmured Adelaide.

Again he scowled, feeling the approach of something hostile to him.

"What's that?" he asked, surmising that she was insulting him.

"I said I supposed you could get a better job if you tried."

He did not like this tone either.

"Well, whether I could or not," he said, "this is no way. I'm losing my hold of my men."

"Oh, I can't imagine your doing that, Burke."

He turned on her to see if she were really daring to laugh at him, and met an eye as steady as his own.

" I guess I'm wasting my time here , " he said, and

something intimated that some one would pay for that expenditure.

"Shall I take a message to Mr. Farron for you?" said Adelaide.

He nodded.

"Yes. Tell him that if I'm to go, I'll go to-day."

"I see." She rose slowly, as if in response to a vague, amusing caprice. "Just that. If you go, you'll go to-day."

For the first time Burke, regaining his self-confidence, saw that she was not an enemy, but an appreciative spectator, and his face broke up in a smile, queer, crooked, wrinkled, but brilliant.

"I guess you'll get it about right," he said, and no compliment had ever pleased Adelaide half so much.

"I think so," she confidently answered, and then at the door she turned. "Oh, Mrs. Baxter," she said, "this is Marty Burke, a very important person."

Importance, especially Adelaide Farron's idea of importance, was a category for which Mrs. Baxter had the highest esteem, so almost against her will she looked at Burke, and found him looking her over with such a shrewd eye that she looked away, and then looked back again to find that his gaze was still upon her. He had made his living since he was a child by his faculty for sizing people up, and at his first glimpse of Mrs. Baxter's shifting glance he had sized her up; so that now, when she remarked with an amiability at once ponderous and shaky that it was a very fine day, he replied in exactly the same tone, "It is that," and began to walk about the room looking at the pictures. Presently a low, but sweet, whistle broke from his lips. He made her feel uncommonly uncomfortable, so uncomfortable that she was driven to conversation.

"Are you fond of pictures, Burke?" she asked. He just looked at her over his shoulder without answering. She began to wish that Adelaide would come back.

Adelaide had found her husband still accessible. He received in silence the announcement that Burke was down-stairs. She told the message without bias.

"He says that they have it on him on the dock that he is to be bounced. He asked me to say this to you: that if he is to go, he'll go to-day."

"What was his manner?"

Adelaide could not resist a note of enjoyment entering into her tone as she replied:

"Insolent in the extreme."

She was leaning against the wall at the foot of his bed, and though she was not looking at him, she felt his eyes on her.

"Adelaide," he said, "you should not have brought me that message."

"You mean it is bad for your health to be worried, dearest?" she asked in a tone so soft that only an expert in tones could have detected something not at all soft beneath it. She glanced at her husband under her lashes. Wasn't he any more an expert in her tones?

"I mean," he answered, "that you should have told him to go to the devil."

"Oh, I leave that to you, Vin." She laughed, and added after a second's pause, "I was only a messenger."

"Tell him I shall be downtown next week."

"Oh, Vin, no; not next week."

"Tell him next week."

"I can't do that."

"I thought you were only a messenger."

"Your doctor would not hear of it. It would be madness."

Farron leaned over and touched his bell. The nurse was instantly in the room, looking at Vincent, Adelaide thought, as a water-dog looks at its master when it perceives that a stick is about to be thrown into the pond.

"Miss Gregory," said Vincent, "there's a young man from my office down-stairs. Will you tell him that I can't see him to-day, but that I shall be down-town next week, and I'll see him then?"

Miss Gregory was almost at the door before Adelaide stopped her.

"You must know that Mr. Farron cannot get downtown next week."

"Has the doctor said not?"

Adelaide shook her head impatiently.

"I don't suppose any one has been so insane as to ask him," she answered.

Miss Gregory smiled temperately.

"Oh, next week is a long time off," she said, and left the room. Adelaide turned to her husband.

"Do you enjoy being humored?" she asked.

Farron had closed his eyes, and now opened them.

"I beg your pardon," he said. "I didn't hear."

"She knows quite well that you can't go downtown next week. She takes your message just to humor you."

"She's an excellent nurse," said Farron.

"For babies," Adelaide felt like answering, but she didn't. She said instead, "Anyhow, Burke will never accept that as an answer." She was surprised to hear something almost boastful in her own tone.

"Oh, I think he will."

She waited breathlessly for some sound from downstairs or even for the flurried reentrance of Miss Gregory. There was a short silence, and then came the sound of the shutting of the front door. Marty had actually gone.

Vincent did not even open his eyes when Miss Gregory returned; he did not exert himself to ask how his message had been received. Adelaide waited an instant, and then went back to Mrs. Baxter with a strange sense of having sustained a small personal defeat.

Mrs. Baxter was so thoroughly ruffled that she was prepared to attack even the sacrosanct Adelaide. But she was not given the chance.

"Well, how did Marty treat you?" said Adelaide.

Mrs. Baxter sniffed.

"We had not very much in common," she returned.

"No; Marty's a very real person." There was a pause. "What became of him? Did he go?"

"Yes, your husband's trained nurse gave him a message, and he went away."

"Quietly?" The note of disappointment was so plain that Mrs. Baxter asked in answer:

"What would you have wanted him to do?"

Adelaide laughed.

"I suppose it would have been too much to expect that he would drag you and Miss Gregory about by your hair," she said, "but I own I should have liked some little demonstration. But perhaps," she added more brightly, "he has gone back to wreck the docks."

At this moment Mathilde entered the room in her hat and furs, and distracted the conversation from Burke. Adelaide, who was fond of enunciating the belief that you could tell when people were in love by the frequency with which they wore their best clothes, noticed now how wonderfully lovely Mathilde was looking; but she noticed it quite unsuspiciously, for she was thinking, "My child is really a beauty."

"You remember Mrs. Baxter, my dear."

Mathilde did not remember her in the least, though she smiled sufficiently. To her Mrs. Baxter seemed just one of many dressy old ladies who drifted across the horizon only too often. If any one had told her that her grandfather had ever been supposed to be in danger of succumbing to charms such as these, she would have thought the notion an ugly example of grown-up pessimism.

Mrs. Baxter held her hand and patted it.

"Where does she get that lovely golden hair?" she asked. "Not from you, does she?"

"She gets it from her father," answered Adelaide, and her expression added, "you dreadful old goose."

In the pause Mathilde made her escape unquestioned. She knew even before a last pathetic glance that her mother was unutterably wearied with her visitor. In other circumstances she would have stayed to effect a rescue, but at present she was engaged in a deed of some recklessness on her own account. She was going to meet Pete Wayne secretly at the Metropolitan Museum.

Alice Duer Miller

CHAPTER XII

In all her life Mathilde had never felt so conspicuous as she did going up the long flight of stairs at the Fifth Avenue entrance of the museum. It seemed to her that people, those walking past in the sunshine on the sidewalk, and the strangers in town seeing the sights from the top of the green busses, were saying to one another as they looked at her, "There goes a New York girl to meet her lover in one of the more ancient of the Egyptian rooms."

She started as she heard the voice of the guard, though he was saying nothing but "Check your umbrella" to a man behind her. She sped across the marble floor of the great tapestry hall as a little, furry wild animal darts across an open space in the woods. She was thinking that she could not bear it if Pete were not there. How could she wait many minutes under the eyes of the guards, who must know better than any one else that no flesh-and-blood girl took any real interest in Egyptian antiquities? The round, unambitious dial at the entrance, like an enlarged kitchen-clock, had pointed to the exact hour set for the meeting. She ought not to expect that Pete, getting away from the office in business hours, could be as punctual as an eager, idle creature like herself.

She had made up her mind so clearly that when she

entered the night-blue room there would be nothing but tombs and mummies that when she saw Pete standing with his overcoat over his arm, in the blue-serge clothes she particularly liked, she felt as much surprised as if their meeting were accidental.

She tried to draw a long breath.

"I shall never get used to it," she said. "If we had been married a thousand years, I should always feel just like this when I see you."

"Oh, no, you won't," he answered. "I hope the very next time we meet you will say, quite in a wife's orthodox tone: 'My dear, I've been waiting twenty minutes. Not that I mind at all; only I was afraid I must have misunderstood you.'"

"You hope? Oh, I hope we shall never be like that."

"Really? Why, I enjoy the idea. I shall enjoy saying to total strangers, 'Ah, gentlemen, if my wife were ever on time - ' It makes me feel so indissolubly united to you."

"I like it best as we are now."

"We might try different methods alternate years: one year we could be domestic, and the next, detached, and so on."

By this time they had discovered that they were leaning on a mummy-case, and Mathilde drew back with an exclamation. "Poor thing!" she said. "I suppose she once had a lover, too."

"And very likely met him in the room of Chinese antiquities in the Temple Museum," said Pete, and then, changing his tone, he added: "But come along. I want to show you a few little things which I have selected to furnish our home. I think you'll like them."

Pete was always inventing games like this, and calling on her to enter in without the slightest warning. One of them was about a fancy ball he was giving in the main hall of the Pennsylvania Station. But this new idea, to treat the whole museum as a sort of super-department store, made her laugh in a faint, dependent way that she knew Pete liked. She believed that such forms of play were peculiar to themselves, so she guarded them as the deepest kind of secret; for she thought, if her mother ever found out about them, she would at once conclude that the whole relation was childish. To all other lovers Mathilde attributed a uniform seriousness.

It took them a long time to choose their house-furnishings: there was a piece of black-and-gold lacquer; a set of painted panels; a Persian rug, swept by the tails of two haughty peacocks; some cloud-gray Chinese porcelains; a set of Du Barry vases; a crystal-and-enamel box, designed probably for some sacred purpose, but contributed by Pete as an excellent receptacle for chocolates at her bedside. "The Boy with the Sword" for the dining-room, Ver Meer's "Women at the Window," the small Bonnington, and then, since Mathilde wanted the portrait of Mrs. Fitzherbert, and Wayne felt a faint weariness with the English school, a compromise was effected by the selection of Constable's landscape of a bridge. Wayne kept constantly repeating that he was exactly like Warren Hastings, astonished at his own moderation. They had hardly begun, indeed, before Mathilde felt herself overcome by that peculiar exhaustion that overtakes even the robust in museums.

Wayne guided her to a little sofa in a room of gold and jade.

"How beautifully you know your way about here!" she said. "I suppose you've brought lots of girls here before me."

"A glorious army," said Pete, "the matron and the maid. You ought to see my mother in a museum. She's lost before she gets well inside the turnstile."

But Mathilde was thinking.

"How strange it is," she observed, "that I never should have thought before about your caring for any one else. Pete, did you ever ask any one else to marry you?"

Wayne nodded.

"Yes; when I was in college. I asked a girl to marry me. She was having rather a rotten time."

"Were you in love with her?"

He shook his head, and in the silence shuffling and staccato footsteps were heard, announcing the approach of a youthful art class and their teacher. "Jade," said the voice of the lady, "one of the hardest of known substances, has yet been beautifully worked from time immemorial -"

More pairs of eyes in that art class were fixed on the obviously guilty couple in the corner than on the beautiful cloudy objects in the cases, and it was not until they had all followed their guide to the armor-room, and had grouped themselves about the casque of Joan of Arc, that Wayne went on as if no interruption had occurred:

"If you want to know whether I have ever experienced anything like my feeling for you since the first moment I saw you, I never have and never shall, and thereto I plight thee my troth."

Mathilde turned her full face toward him, shedding gratitude and affection as a lamp sheds light before she answered:

"You were terribly unkind to me yesterday."

"I know. I'm sorry."

"I shall never forget the way you kissed me, as if I were a rather repulsive piece of wood."

Pete craned his neck, and met the suspicious eye of a guard.

"I don't think anything can be done about it at the moment," he said; and added in explanation, "You see, I felt as if you had suddenly deserted me."

"Pete, I couldn't ever desert you - unless I committed suicide."

Presently he stood up, declaring that this was not the fitting place for arranging the details of their marriage.

"Come to one of the smaller picture galleries," he said,

"and as we go I'll show you a portrait of my mother."

"Your mother? I did not know she had had a portrait done. By whom?"

"A fellow called Bellini. He thought he was doing the Madonna."

When they reached the picture, a figure was already before it. Mr. Lanley was sitting, with his arms folded and his feet stretched out far before him, his head bent, but his eyes raised and fixed on the picture. They saw him first, and had two or three seconds to take in the profound contemplation of his mood. Then he slowly raised his eyes and encountered theirs.

There is surely nothing compromising in an elderly gentleman spending a contemplative morning alone at the Metropolitan Museum. It might well be his daily custom; but the knowledge that it was not, the consciousness of the rarity of the mood that had brought him there, oppressed Mr. Lanley almost like a crime. He felt caught, outraged, ashamed as he saw them. "That's the age which has a right to it," he said to himself. And then as if in a mirror he saw an expression of embarrassment on their faces, and was reminded that their meeting must have been illicit, too. He stood up and looked at them sternly.

"Up-town at this hour, Wayne?" he said.

"Grandfather, I never knew you came here much," said Mathilde.

"It's near me, you know," he answered weakly, so weakly that he felt impelled to give an explanation.

"Sometimes, my dear," he said, "you will find that even the most welcome guest rather fills the house."

"You need not worry about yours," returned Mathilde. "I left her with Mama."

Mr. Lanley felt that his brief moment of peace was indeed over. He could imagine the impressions that Mrs. Baxter was perhaps at that very moment sharing with Adelaide. He longed to question his granddaughter, but did not know how to put it.

"How was your mother looking?" he finally decided upon.

"Dreary," answered Mathilde, with a laugh.

"Does this picture remind you of any one?" asked Wayne, suddenly.

Mr. Lanley looked at him as if he hadn't heard, and frowned.

"I don't know what you mean," he said.

"Don't you think there's a look of my mother about it?"

"No," said Mr. Lanley, rather loudly, and then added, "Well, I see what you mean, though I shouldn't -" He stopped and turning to them with some sternness, he asked them how they accounted for their presence in the museum at such an hour and alone.

There was nothing to do but to tell him the truth. And when Wayne had finished, Mathilde was surprised at her grandfather's question. She thought he would ask what her mother thought of it. If they had been alone, she would have told him that Adelaide thought Wayne a commonplace young man with stubby hands; but as it was, she had resolved to put her mother's opposition on a more dignified plane. Only Mr. Lanley did not ask the question of her. It was to Wayne he was speaking, when he said:

"What does your mother think of it?"

"Oh, my mother," answered Pete. "Well, she thinks that if she were a girl she'd like to go to China."

Mr. Lanley looked up, and they both smiled with the most perfect understanding.

"She would," said the older man, and then he became intensely serious. "It's quite out of the question," he said.

"O Grandfather," Mathilde exclaimed, clasping her hands about his arm, "don't talk like that! It wouldn't be possible for me to let him go without me. O Grandfather, can't you remember what it was like to be in love?"

A complete silence followed this little speech - a silence that went on and on and seemed to be stronger than human power. Perhaps for the first time in his life Lanley felt hostile toward the girl beside him. "Oh, dear," Mathilde was thinking, "I suppose I've made him remember my grandmother and his youth!" "Can love be remembered," Pete was saying to himself, "or is it like a perfume that can be recognized, but not recalled?"

Lanley turned at last to Wayne.

"It's out of the question," he said, "that you should take this child to China at two weeks' notice. You must see that."

"I see perfectly that many people will think it so. But you must see that to us it is the inevitable thing to do."

"If every one else agreed, I should oppose it."

"O Grandfather!" wailed Mathilde. "And you were our great hope - you and Mrs. Wayne!"

"In a matter like this I shall stand by your mother, Mathilde," he said, and Mathilde imagined he meant as opposed to herself. But he was making an even greater renunciation.

Adelaide was surprised and not pleased when Mathilde came home late for lunch, bringing the Wayne boy with her. It was not that she had expected her one little phrase about Wayne's hands to change her daughter's love into repugnance, - that sentence had been only the first drop in a distillation that would do its poisonous work gradually, - but she had supposed that Mathilde would be too sensitive to expose Pete to further criticism. Indeed, there seemed something obtuse, if not actually indelicate, in being willing to create a situation in which every one was bound to suffer. Obtuseness was not a defect with which Adelaide had much patience.

Mathilde saw at once that her mother was going to be what in the family slang was called "grand." The grandeur consisted in a polite inattention; it went with a soft voice and immobile expression. In this mood Adelaide answered you about three seconds later than you expected, and though she answered you accurately, it was as if she had forced her mind back from a more congenial ether. She seemed to be wrapped in an agreeable cloud until you gave her some opening, and then she came out of her cloud like a flash of lightning.

Wayne, who had lived his life so far with a woman who did not believe in the use of force in human relations, viewed these symptoms of coercion with the utmost indifference; but Mathilde had not so far freed herself as to ignore them. She was not afraid, but easy conversation under the menace was beyond her. She couldn't think of anything to say.

Adelaide was accustomed by these methods to drive the inexperienced - and she considered Pete pitifully inexperienced in social fine points - into a state of conversational unrest in which they would finally ask recklessly, "Have you been to the theater lately?" and she would question gently, "The theater?" as much as to say, "I've heard that word somewhere before," until the conscientious conversationalist, rushing from futility to futility, would be finally engulfed in some yawning banality and sink out of sight forever.

But Wayne resisted this temptation, or, rather, he did not feel it. He had the courage to be unafraid of silences, and he ate his luncheon and thought about the pictures he had been seeing, and at last began to talk to Mathilde about them, while Adelaide made it clear that she was not listening, until she caught a phrase that drove her grandeur away.

"Near where we met my grandfather?" Mathilde asked.

By this time Adelaide had gathered that the two had been in the museum, and the knowledge annoyed her not only as a mother, but as an aristocrat. Without being clear about it, she regarded the love of beauty - artificial beauty, that is - as a class distinction. It seemed to her possible enough that the masses should love mountains and moonlight and the sea and sunsets; but it struck her as unfitting that any one but the people she knew, and only a few of them, should really care for porcelains and pictures. As she held herself aloof from the conversation she was annoyed at noticing that Wayne was showing a more discriminating taste than her own carefully nurtured child. But all such considerations were driven away by the mention of her father, for Mr. Lanley had been in her mind ever since Mrs. Baxter had taken her unimpeded departure just before luncheon.

"Your grandfather?" she said, coming out of the clouds. "Was he in the Metropolitan?"

"Yes," said Mathilde, thankful to be directly addressed. "Wasn't it queer? Pete was taking me to see a picture that looks exactly like Mrs. Wayne, only Mrs. Wayne hasn't such a round face, and there in front of it was grandpapa."

Adelaide rose very slowly from table, lunch being fortunately over. She felt as if she could have borne almost anything but this - the idea of her father vaporing before a picture of the Madonna. Phrases came into her head: silly old man, the time has come to protect him against himself; the Wayne family must be suppressed.

Her silence in the drawing-room was of a more concentrated sort, and when she had taken her coffee and cigarette she said to Mathilde:

"My dear, I promised to go back to Vincent at this time. Will you go instead? I want to have a word with Mr. Wayne."

Adelaide had never entered any contest in her life, whether it was a dispute with a dressmaker or a quarrel with her husband, without remembering the comfortable fact that she was a beauty. With men she did not neglect the advantage that being a woman gave her, and with the particular man now before her she had, she knew, a third line of defense; she was the mother of his love, and she thought she detected in him a special weakness for mothers. But it would have been better if he had respected women and mothers less, for he thought so highly of them that he believed they ought to play fair.

Sitting in a very low chair, she looked up at him.

"Mathilde has been telling me something about a plan of yours to take her to China with you. We could not consent to that, you know."

"I'm sorry," said Pete. The tone was pleasant. That was the trouble; it was too pleasant a tone for a man relinquishing a cherished hope. It sounded almost as if he regretted the inevitable disappointment of the family.

Adelaide tried a new attack.

"Your mother - have you consulted her?"

Alice Duer Miller

"Yes, I've told her our plans."

"And she approves?"

Wayne might choose to betray his mother in the full irresponsibility of her attitude to so sympathetic a listener as Mr. Lanley, but he had no intention of giving Mrs. Farron such a weapon. At the same time he did not intend to be untruthful. His answer was this:

"My mother," he said, "is not like most women of her age. She believes in love."

"In all love, quite indiscriminately?"

He hesitated an instant.

"I put it wrong," he answered. "I meant that she believes in the importance of real love."

"And has she a spell by which she tells real love?"

"She believes mine to be real."

"Oh, yours! Very likely. Perhaps it's maternal vanity on my part, Mr. Wayne, but I must own I can imagine a man's contriving to love my daughter, so gentle, so intelligent, and so extraordinarily lovely to look at. I was not thinking of your feelings, but of hers."

"You can see no reason why she should love me?"

Adelaide moved her shoulders about.

"Well, I want it explained, that's all, from your own point of view. I see my daughter as an unusual person, ignorant of life, to whom it seems to me all things are possible. And I see you, a very nice young man. But what else? I ask to be told why you fulfil all possibilities. Don't misunderstand me. I am not mercenary. Mathilde will have plenty of money of her own some day. I don't want a millionaire. I want a *person*."

"Of course, if you ask me why Mathilde should love me -"

"Don't be untruthful, Mr. Wayne. I thought better of you. If you should come back from China next year to find her engaged to some one else, you could tell a great many reasons why he was not good enough for her. Now tell me some of the reasons why you are. And please don't include because you love her so much, for almost any one would do that."

Pete fought down his panic, reminding himself that no man living could hear such words without terror. His egotism, never colossal, stood feebly between him and Mrs. Farron's estimate of him. He seemed to sink back into the general human species. If he had felt inclined to detail his own qualities, he could not have thought of one. There was a long silence, while Adelaide sat with a look of docile teachableness upon her expectant face.

At last Wayne stood up.

"It's no use, Mrs. Farron," he said "That question of yours can't be answered. I believe she loves me. It's my bet against yours."

"I won't gamble with my child's future," she returned.

"I did with my own. Sit down again, Mr. Wayne. You have heard, I suppose, that I have been married twice?"

"Yes." He sat down again reluctantly.

"I was Mathilde's age - a little older. I was more in love than she. And if he had been asked the question I just asked you, he could have answered it. He could have said: 'I have been a leader in a group in which I was, an athlete, an oarsman, and the most superb physical specimen of my race' - brought up, too, he might have added, in the same traditions that I had had. Well, that wasn't enough, Mr. Wayne, and that was a good deal. If my father had only made me wait, only given me time to see that my choice was the choice of ignorance, that the man I thought a hero was, oh, the most pitifully commonplace clay - Mathilde shan't make my mistake."

Wayne's eyes lit up.

"But that's it," he said. "She wouldn't make your mistake. She'd choose right. That's what I ought to have said. You spoke of Mathilde's spirit. She has a feeling for the right thing. Some people have, and some people are bound to choose wrong."

Adelaide laid her hand on her breast.

"You mean me?" she asked, too much interested to be angry.

He was too absorbed in his own interests to give his full attention to hers.

"Yes," he answered. "I mean your principles of choice

weren't right ones - leaders of men, you know, and all that. It never works out. Leaders of men are the ones who always cry on their wives' shoulders, and the martinets at home are imposed on by every one else." He gave out this dictum in passing: "But don't trouble about your responsibility in this, Mrs. Farron. It's out of your hands. It's our chance, and Mathilde and I mean to take it. I don't want to give you a warning, exactly, but - it's going to go through."

She looked at him with large, terrified eyes. She was repeating, 'they cry on their wives' shoulders,' or, he might have said, 'on the shoulders of their trained nurses.' She knew that he was talking to her, saying something. She couldn't listen to it. And then he was gone. She was glad he was.

She sat quite still, with her hands lying idly, softly in her lap. It was possible that what he said was true. Perhaps all these people who made such a show of strength to the world were those who sucked double strength by sapping the vitality of a life's companion. It had been true of Joe Severance. She had heard him praised for the courage with which he went forth against temptation, but she had known that it was her strength he was using. She looked up, to see her daughter, pale and eager, standing before her.

"O Mama, was it very terrible?"

"What, dear?"

"Did Pete tell you of our plan?"

Adelaide wished she could have listened to those last sentences of his; but they were gone completely.

She put up her hand and patted the unutterably soft cheek before her.

"He told me something about putting through your absurd idea of an immediate marriage," she said.

"We don't want to do it in a sneaky way, Mama."

"I know. You want to have your own way and to have every one approve of you, too. Is that it?"

Mathilde's lips trembled.

"O Mama," she cried, "you are so different from what you used to be!"

Adelaide nodded.

"One changes," she said. "One's life changes." She had meant this sentence to end the interview, but when she saw the girl still standing before her, she said to herself that it made little difference that she hadn't heard the plans of the Wayne boy, since Mathilde, her own tractable daughter, was still within her power. She moved into the corner of the sofa. "Sit down, dear," she said, and when Mathilde had obeyed with an almost imperceptible shrinking in her attitude, Adelaide went on, with a sort of serious ease of manner:

"I've never been a particularly flattering mother, have I? Never thought you were perfect just because you were mine? Well, I hope you'll pay the more attention to what I have to say. You are remarkable. You are going to be one of the most attractive women that ever was. Years ago old Count Bartiani - do you remember him, at Lucerne?"

"The one who used scent and used to look so long at me?"

"Yes, he was old and rather horrid, but he knew what he was talking about. He said then you would be the most attractive woman in Europe. I heard the same thing from all my friends, and it's true. You have something rare and perfect -"

These were great words. Mathilde, accustomed all her life to receive information from her mother, received this; and for the first time felt the egotism of her beauty awake, a sense of her own importance the more vivid because she had always been humble-minded. She did not look at her mother; she sat up very straight and stared as if at new fields before her, while a faint smile flickered at the corners of her mouth - a smile of an awakening sense of power.

"What you have," Adelaide went on, "ought to bring great happiness, great position, great love; and how can I let you throw yourself away at eighteen on a commonplace boy with a glib tongue and a high opinion of himself? Don't tell me that it will make you happy. That would be the worst of all, if you turned out to be so limited that you were satisfied, - that would be a living death. O my darling, I give you my word that if you will give up this idea, ten years from now, when you see this boy, still glib, still vain, and perhaps a little fat, you will actually shudder when you think how near he came to cutting you off from the wonderful, full life that you were entitled to." And then, as if she could not hope to better this, Adelaide sprang up, and left the girl alone.

Mathilde rose, too, and looked at herself in the glass. She was stirred, she was changed, she was awakened, but awakened to something her mother had not counted on. Almost too gentle, too humble, too reasonable, as she had always been, the drop of egotism which her mother had succeeded in instilling into her nature served to solidify her will, to inspire her with a needed power of aggression.

She nodded once at her image in the mirror.

"Well," she said, "it's my life, and I'm willing to take the consequences."

CHAPTER XIII

When Mathilde emerged from the subway into the sunlight of City Hall Park, Pete was nowhere to be seen. She had spent several minutes wandering in the subterranean labyrinth which threatened to bring her to Brooklyn Bridge and nowhere else, so she was a little late for her appointment; and yet Pete was not there. He had promised to be waiting for her. This was a more important occasion than the meeting in the museum and more terrifying, too.

Their plans were simple. They were going to get their marriage license, they were going to be married immediately, they were then going to inform their respective families, and start two days later for San Francisco.

Mathilde stared furtively about her. A policeman strolled past, striking terror to a guilty heart; a gentleman of evidently unbroken leisure regarded her with a benevolent eye completely ringed by red. Crowds were surging in and out of the newspaper offices and the Municipal Building and the post office, but stare where she would, she couldn't find Pete.

She had ten minutes to think of horrors before she saw him rushing across the park toward her, and she had the idea of saying to him those words which he himself

Alice Duer Miller

had selected as typically wifely, "Not that I mind at all, but I was afraid I must have misunderstood you." But she did not get very far in her mild little joke, for it was evident at once that something had happened.

"My dear love," he said, "it's no go. We can't sail, we can't be married. I think I'm out of a job."

As they stood there, her pretty clothes, the bright sun shining on her golden hair and dark furs and polished shoes, her beauty, but, above all, their complete absorption in each other, made them conspicuous. They were utterly oblivious.

Pete told her exactly what had happened. Some months before he had been sent to make a report on a coal property in Pennsylvania. He had made it under the assumption that the firm was thinking of underwriting its bonds. He had been mistaken. As owners Honaton & Benson had already acquired the majority of interest in it. His report, - she remembered his report, for he had told her about it the first day he came to see her, - had been favorable except for one important fact. There was in that district a car shortage which for at least a year would hamper the marketing of the supply. That had been the point of the whole thing. He had advised against taking the property over until this defect could be remedied or allowed for. They had accepted the report.

Well, late in the afternoon of the preceding day he had gone to the office to say good-by to the firm. He could not help being touched by the friendliness of both men's manner. Honaton gave him a silver traveling-flask, plain except for an offensive cat's-eye set in the top. Benson, more humane and practical, gave him a check.

"I think I've cleared up everything before I leave," Wayne said, trying to be conscientious in return for their kindness, "except one thing. I've never corrected the proof of my report on the Southerland coal property."

For a second there was something strange in the air. The partners exchanged the merest flicker of a look, which Wayne, as far as he thought of it at all, supposed to be a recognition on their part of his carefulness in thinking of such a detail.

"You need not give that another thought," said Benson. "We are not thinking of publishing that report at present. And when we do, I have your manuscript. I'll go over the proof myself."

Relieved to be spared another task, Wayne shook hands with his employers and withdrew. Outside he met David.

"Say," said David, "I am sorry you're leaving us; but, gee!" he added, his face twisting with joy, "ain't the firm glad to have you go!"

It had long been Wayne's habit to pay strict attention to the impressions of David.

"Why do you think they are glad?" he asked.

"Oh, they're glad all right," said David. "I heard the old man say yesterday, 'And by next Saturday he will be at sea.' It was as if he was going to get a Christmas present." And David went on about other business.

Once put on the right track, it was not difficult to get the idea. He went to the firm's printer, but found they had had no orders for printing his report. The next morning, instead of spending his time with his own last arrangements, he began hunting up other printing offices, and finally found what he was looking for. His report was already in print, with one paragraph left out - that one which related to the shortage of cars. His name was signed to it, with a little preamble by the firm, urging the investment on the favorable notice of their customers, and spoke in high terms of the accuracy of his estimates.

To say that Pete did not once contemplate continuing his arrangements as if nothing had happened would not be true. All he had to do was to go. The thing was dishonest, clearly enough, but it was not his action. His original report would always be proof of his own integrity, and on his return he could sever his connection with the firm on some other pretext. On the other hand, to break his connection with Honaton & Benson, to force the suppression of the report unless given in full, to give up his trip, to confess that immediate marriage was impossible, that he himself was out of a job, that the whole basis of his good fortune was a fraud that he had been too stupid to discover - all this seemed to him more than man could be asked to do.

But that was what he decided must be done. From the printer's he telephoned to the Farrons, but found that Miss Severance was out. He knew she must have already started for their appointment in the City Hall Park. He had made up his mind, and yet when he saw her, so confident of the next step, waiting for him, he very nearly yielded to a sudden temptation to make her his wife, to be sure of that, whatever else might have to be altered.

He had known she wouldn't reproach him, but he was deeply grateful to her for being so unaware that there was any grounds for reproach. She understood the courage his renunciation had required. That seemed to be what she cared for most.

At length he said to her:

"Now I must go and get this off my chest with the firm. Go home, and I'll come as soon as ever I can."

But here she shook her head.

"I couldn't go home," she answered. "It might all come out before you arrived, and I could not listen to things that" - she avoided naming her mother - "that will be said about you, Pete. Isn't there somewhere I can wait while you have your interview?"

There was the outer office of Honaton & Benson. He let her go with him, and turned her over to the care of David, who found her a corner out of the way, and left her only once. That was to say to a friend of his in the cage: "When you go out, cast your eye over Pete's girl. Somewhat of a peacherino."

In the meantime Wayne went into Benson's office. There wasn't a flicker of alarm on the senior partner's face on seeing him.

"Hullo, Pete!" he said, "I thought you'd be packing your bags."

"I'm not packing anything," said Wayne. "I've come to tell you I can't go to China for you. Mr. Benson."

"Oh, come, come," said the other, very paternally, "we can't let you off like that. This is business, my dear boy. It would cost us money, after having made all our arrangements, if you changed your mind."

"So I understand."

"What do you mean?"

"I mean just what you think I mean, Mr. Benson."

Wayne would have said that he could never forget the presence under any circumstances of his future wife, waiting, probably nervously, in the outer office; but he did. The interest of the next hour drove out everything else. Honaton was sent for from the exchange, a lawsuit was threatened, a bribe - he couldn't mistake it - offered. He was told he might find it difficult to find another position if he left their firm under such conditions.

"On the contrary," said Peter, firmly, "from what I have heard, I believe it will improve my standing."

That he came off well in the struggle was due not so much to his ability, but to the fact that he now had nothing to lose or gain from the situation. As soon as Benson grasped this fact he began a masterly retreat. Wayne noticed the difference between the partners: Honaton, the less able of the two, wanted to save the situation, but before everything else wanted to leave in Wayne's mind the sense that he had made a fool of himself. Benson, more practical, would have been glad to put Pete in jail if he could; but as he couldn't do that, his interest was in nothing but saving the situation. The only way to do this was to give up all idea of publishing any report. He did this by assuming that Wayne had simply changed his mind or had at least utterly failed to convey his meaning in his written words. He made this point of view very plausible by quoting the more laudatory of Wayne's sentences; and when Pete explained that the whole point of his report was in the sentence that had been omitted, Benson leaned back, chuckling, and biting off the end of his cigar.

"Oh, you college men!" he said. "I'm afraid I'm not up to your subtleties. When you said it was the richest vein and favorably situated, I supposed that was what you meant. If you meant just the opposite, well, let it go. Honaton & Benson certainly don't want to get out a report contrary to fact."

"That's what he has accused us of," said Honaton.

"Oh, no, no," said Benson; "don't be too literal, Jack. In the heat of argument we all say things we don't mean. Pete here doesn't like to have his lovely English all messed up by a practical dub like me. I doubt if he wants to sever his connection with this firm."

Honaton yielded.

"Oh," he said, "I'm willing enough he should stay, if -"

"Well, I'm not," said Pete, and put an end to the conversation by walking out of the room. He found David explaining the filing system to Mathilde, and she, hanging on his every word, partly on account of his native charm, partly on account of her own interest in anything neat, but most because she imagined the knowledge might some day make her a more serviceable wife to Pete.

Pete dreaded the coming interview with Mrs. Farron more than that with the firm - more, indeed, than he had ever dreaded anything. He and Mathilde reached the house about a quarter before one, and Adelaide was not in. This was fortunate, for while they waited they discovered a difference of intention. Mathilde saw no reason for mentioning the fact that they had actually been on the point of taking out their marriage license. She thought it was enough to tell her mother that the trip had been abandoned and that Pete had given up his job. Pete contemplated nothing less than the whole truth.

"You can't tell people half a story," he said. "It never works."

Mathilde really quailed.

"It will be terrible to tell mama that," she groaned. "She thinks failure is worse than crime."

"And she's dead right," said Pete.

When Adelaide came in she had Mr. Lanley with her. She had seen him walking down Fifth Avenue with his hat at quite an outrageous angle, and she had ordered the motor to stop, and had beckoned him to her. It was two days since her interview with Mrs. Baxter, and she had had no good opportunity of speaking to him. The suspicion that he was avoiding her nerved her hand; but there was no hint of discipline in her smile, and she knew as well as if he had said it that he was thinking as he came to the side of the car how handsome and how creditable a daughter she was. "Come to lunch with me," she said; "or must you go home to your guest?"

"No, I was going to the club. She's lunching with a mysterious relation near Columbia University."

"Don't you know who it is? Tell him home."

"Home, Andrews. No, she never says."

"Don't put your stick against the glass, there's an angel. I'll tell you who it is. An elder sister who supported and educated her, of whom she's ashamed now."

"How do you know? It wouldn't break the glass."

"No; but I hate the noise. I don't know; I just made it up because it's so likely."

"She always speaks so affectionately of you."

"She's a coward; that's the only difference. She hates me just as much."

"Well, you've never been nice to her, Adelaide."

"I should think not."

"She's not as bad as you think," said Mr. Lanley, who believed in old-fashioned loyalty.

"I can't bear her," said Adelaide.

"Why not?" As far as his feelings went, this seemed a

perfectly safe question; but it wasn't.

"Because she tries so hard to make you ridiculous. Oh, not intentionally; but she talks of you as if you were a *Don Juan* of twenty-five. You ought to be flattered, Papa dear, at having jealous scenes made about you when you are - what is it? - sixty-five."

"Four," said Mr. Lanley.

"Yes; such a morning as I had! Not a minute with poor Vincent because you had had Mrs. Wayne to dine. I'm not complaining, but I don't like my father represented as a sort of comic-paper old man, you poor dear," - and she laid her long, gloved hand on his knee, - "who have always been so conspicuously dignified."

"If I have," said her father, "I don't know that anything she says can change it."

"No, of course; only it was horrible to me to hear her describing you in the grip of a boyish passion. But don't let's talk of it. I hear," she said, as if she were changing the subject, "that you have taken to going to the Metropolitan Museum at odd moments."

He felt utterly stripped, and said without hope:

"Yes; I'm a trustee, you know."

Adelaide just glanced at him.

"You always have been, I think." They drove home in silence.

One reason why she was determined to have her father

come home was that it was the first time that Vincent was to take luncheon downstairs, and when Adelaide had a part to play she liked to have an audience. She was even glad to find Wayne in the drawing-room, though she did wonder to herself if the little creature had entirely given up earning his living. It was a very different occasion from Pete's last luncheon there; every one was as pleasant as possible. As soon as the meal was over, Adelaide put her hand on her husband's shoulder.

"You're going to lie down at once, Vin."

He rose obediently, but Wayne interposed. It seemed to him that it would be possible to tell his story to Farron.

"Oh, can't Mr. Farron stay a few minutes?" he said. "I want so much to speak to you and him together about -"

Adelaide cut him short.

"No, he can't. It's more important that he should get strong than anything else is. You can talk to me all you like when I come down. Come, Vin."

When they were up-stairs, and she was tucking him up on his sofa, he asked gently:

"What did that boy want?"

Adelaide made a little face.

"Nothing of any importance," she said.

Things had indeed changed between them if he would accept such an answer as that. She thought his indifference like the studied oblivion of the debtor who says, "Don't I owe you something?" and is content with the most non-committal reply. He lay back and smiled at her. His expression was not easy to read.

She went down-stairs, where conversation had not prospered. Mr. Lanley was smoking, with his cigar drooping from a corner of his mouth. He felt very unhappy. Mathilde was frightened. Wayne had recast his opening sentence a dozen times. He kept saying to himself that he wanted it to be perfectly simple, but not infantile, and each phrase he thought of in conformity with his one rule sounded like the opening lines of the stage child's speech.

In the crisis of Adelaide's being actually back again in the room he found himself saying:

"Mrs. Farron, I think you ought to know exactly what has been happening."

"Don't I?" she asked.

"No. You know that I was going to San Francisco the day after to-morrow -"

"Oh dear," said Adelaide, regretfully, "is it given up?"

He told her rather slowly the whole story. The most terrible moment was, as he had expected, when he explained that they had met, he and Mathilde, to apply for their marriage license. Adelaide turned, and looked full at her daughter.

"You were going to treat me like that?" Mathilde burst into tears. She had long been on the brink of them, and now they came more from nerves than from a sense of the justice of her mother's complaint. But the sound of them upset Wayne hopelessly. He couldn't go on for a minute, and Mr. Lanley rose to his feet.

"Good Lord! good Lord!" he said, "that was dishonorable! Can't you see that that is dishonorable, to marry her on the sly when we trusted her to go about with you -"

"O Papa, never mind about the dishonorableness," said Adelaide. "The point is" - and she looked at Wayne "that they were building their elopement on something that turned out to be a fraud. That doesn't make one think very highly of your judgment, Mr. Wayne."

"I made a mistake, Mrs. Farron."

"It was a bad moment to make one. You have worked three years with this firm and never suspected anything wrong?"

"Yes, sometimes I have -"

Adelaide's eyebrows went up.

"Oh, you have suspected. You had reason to think the whole thing might be dishonest, but you were willing to run away with Mathilde and let her get inextricably committed before you found out -"

"That's irresponsible, sir," said Lanley. "I don't suppose you understood what you were doing, but it was utterly irresponsible."

"I think," said Adelaide, "that it finally answers the question as to whether or not you are too young to be married."

"Mama, I will marry Pete," said Mathilde, trying to make a voice broken with sobs sound firm and resolute.

"Mr. Wayne at the moment has no means whatsoever, as I understand it," said Adelaide.

"I don't care whether he has or not," said Mathilde.

Adelaide laughed. The laugh rather shocked Mr. Lanley. He tried to explain.

"I feel sorry for you, but you can't imagine how painful it is to us to think that Mathilde came so near to being mixed up with a crooked deal like that - Mathilde, of all people. You ought to see that for yourself."

"I see it, thank you," said Pete.

"Really, Mr. Wayne, I don't think that's quite the tone to take," put in Adelaide.

"I don't think it is," said Wayne.

Mathilde, making one last grasp at self-control, said:

"They wouldn't be so horrid to you, Pete, if they understood -" But the muscles of her throat contracted, and she never got any further.

"I suppose I shall be thought a very cruel parent," said

Adelaide, almost airily, "but this sort of thing can't go on, really, you know."

"No, it really can't," said Mr. Lanley. "We feel you have abused our confidence."

"No, I don't reproach Mr. Wayne along those lines," said Adelaide. "He owes me nothing. I had not supposed Mathilde would deceive me, but we won't discuss that now. It isn't anything against Mr. Wayne to say he has made a mistake. Five years from now, I'm sure, he would not put himself, or let himself be put, in such an extremely humiliating position. And I don't say that if he came back five years from now with some financial standing I should be any more opposed to him than to any one else. Only in the meantime there can be no engagement." Adelaide looked very reasonable. "You must see that."

"You mean I'm not to see him?"

"Of course not."

"I must see him," said Mathilde.

Lanley looked at Wayne.

"This is an opportunity for you to rehabilitate yourself. You ought to be man enough to promise you won't see her until you are in a position to ask her to be your wife."

"I have asked her that already, you know," returned Wayne with an attempt at a smile.

"Pete, you wouldn't desert me?" said Mathilde.

"If Mr. Wayne had any pride, my dear, he would not wish to come to a house where he was unwelcome," said her mother.

"I'm afraid I haven't any of that sort of pride at all, Mrs. Farron."

Adelaide made a little gesture, as much as to say, with her traditions, she really did not know how to deal with people who hadn't.

"Mathilde," - Wayne spoke very gently, - "don't you think you could stop crying?"

"I'm trying all the time, Pete. You won't go away, no matter what they say?"

"Of course not."

"It seems to be a question between what I think best for my daughter as opposed to what you think best - for yourself," observed Adelaide.

"Nobody wants to turn you out of the house, you know," said Mr. Lanley in a conciliatory tone, "but the engagement is at an end."

"If you do turn him out, I'll go with him," said Mathilde, and she took his hand and held it in a tight, moist clasp.

They looked so young and so distressed as they stood there hand in hand that Lanley found himself relenting.

"We don't say that your marriage will never be possible," he said. "We are asking you to wait - consent to a separation of six months."

"Six months!" wailed Mathilde.

"With your whole life before you?" her grandfather returned wistfully.

"I'm afraid I am asking a little more than that, Papa," said Adelaide. "I have never been enthusiastic about this engagement, but while I was watching and trying to be cooperative, it seems Mr. Wayne intended to run off with my daughter. I know Mathilde is young and easily influenced, but I don't think, I don't really think," - Adelaide made it evident that she was being just, - "that any other of all the young men who come to the house would have tried to do that, and none of them would have got themselves into this difficulty. I mean," - she looked up at Wayne, - "I think almost any of them would have had a little better business judgment than you have shown."

"Mama," put in her daughter, "can't you see how honest it was of Pete not to go, anyhow?"

Adelaide smiled ironically.

"No; I can't think that an unusually high standard, dear."

This seemed to represent the final outrage to Mathilde. She turned.

"O Pete, wouldn't your mother take me in?" she asked.

And as if to answer the question, Pringle opened the door and announced Mrs. Wayne.

CHAPTER XIV

In all the short, but crowded, time since Lanley had first known Mrs. Wayne he had never been otherwise than glad to see her, but now his heart sank. It seemed to him that an abyss was about to open between them, and that all their differences of spirit, stimulating enough while they remained in the abstract, were about to be cast into concrete form.

Mathilde and Pete were so glad to see her that they said nothing, but looked at her beamingly. Whatever Adelaide's feelings may have been, she greeted her guest with a positive courtesy, and she was the only one who did.

Mrs. Wayne nodded to her son, smiled more formally at Mr. Lanley, and then her eyes falling upon Mathilde, she realized that she had intruded on some sort of conference. She had a natural dread of such meetings, at which it seemed to her that the only thing which she must not do was the only thing that she knew how to do, namely, to speak her mind. So she at once decided to withdraw.

"Your man insisted on my coming in, Mrs. Farron," she said. "I came to ask about Mr. Farron; but I see you are in the midst of a family discussion, and so I won't -"

Everybody separately cried out to her to stay as she began to retreat to the door, and no one more firmly than Adelaide, who thought it as careless as Mr. Lanley thought it creditable that a mother would be willing to go away and leave the discussion of her son's life to others. Adelaide saw an opportunity of killing two birds.

"You are just the person for whom I have been longing, Mrs. Wayne," she said. "Now you have come, we can settle the whole question."

"And just what is the question?" asked Mrs. Wayne. She sat down, looking distressed and rather guilty. She knew they were going to ask her what she knew about all the things that had been going on, and a hasty examination of her consciousness showed her that she knew everything, though she had avoided Pete's full confidence. She knew simply by knowing that any two young people who loved each other would rather marry than separate for a year. But she was aware that this deduction, so inevitable to her, was exactly the one which would be denied by the others. So she sat, with a nervously pleasant smile on her usually untroubled face, and waited for Adelaide to speak. She did not have long to wait.

"You did not know, I am sure, Mrs. Wayne, that your son intended to run away with my daughter?"

All four of them stared at her, making her feel more and more guilty; and at last Lanley, unable to bear it, asked:

"Did you know that, Mrs. Wayne?"

"Oh, dear!" said Mrs. Wayne. "Yes. I knew it was possible; so did you. Pete didn't tell me about it, though."

"But I did tell Mrs. Farron," said Pete.

Adelaide protested at once.

"You told me?" Then she remembered that a cloud had obscured the end of their last interview, but she did not withdraw her protest.

"You know, Mrs. Farron, you have a bad habit of not listening to what is said to you," Wayne answered firmly.

This sort of impersonal criticism was to Adelaide the greatest impertinence, and she showed her annoyance.

"In spite of the disabilities of age, Mr. Wayne," she said, "I find I usually can get a simple idea if clearly presented."

"Why, how absurd that is, Wayne!" put in Mr. Lanley. "You don't mean to say that you told Mrs. Farron you were going to elope with her daughter, and she didn't take in what you said?"

"And yet that is just what took place."

Adelaide glanced at her father, as much as to say, "You see what kind of young man it is," and then went on:

"One fact at least I have learned only this minute - that is that the finances for this romantic trip were to be furnished by a dishonorable firm from which your son has been dismissed; or, no, resigned, isn't it?"

The human interest attached to losing a job brought mother and son together on the instant.

"O Pete, you've left the firm!"

He nodded.

"O my poor boy!"

He made a gesture, indicating that this was not the time to discuss the economic situation, and Adelaide went smoothly on:

"And now, Mrs. Wayne, the point is this. I am considered harsh because I insist that a young man without an income who has just come near to running off with my child on money that was almost a bribe is not a person in whom I have unlimited confidence. I ask - it seems a tolerably mild request - that they do not see each other for six months."

"I cannot agree to that," said Wayne decidedly.

"Really, Mr. Wayne, do you feel yourself in a position to agree or disagree? We have never consented to your engagement. We have never thought the marriage a suitable one, have we, Papa?"

"No," said Mr. Lanley in a tone strangely dead.

"Why is it not suitable?" asked Mrs. Wayne, as if she really hoped that an agreement might be reached by rational discussion.

"Why?" said Adelaide, and smiled. "Dear Mrs. Wayne, these things are rather difficult to explain. Wouldn't it be easier for all of us if you would just accept the statement that we think so without trying to decide whether we are right or wrong?"

"I'm afraid it must be discussed," answered Mrs. Wayne.

Adelaide leaned back, still with her faint smile, as if defying, though very politely, any one to discuss it with *her*.

It was inevitable that Mrs. Wayne should turn to Mr. Lanley.

"You, too, think it unsuitable?"

He bowed gravely.

"You dislike my son?"

"Quite the contrary."

"Then you must be able to tell me the reason."

"I will try," he said. He felt like a soldier called upon to defend a lost cause. It was his cause, he couldn't desert it. His daughter and his granddaughter needed his protection; but he knew he was giving up something that he valued more than his life as he began to speak. "We feel the difference in background," he said, "of early traditions, of judging life from the same point of view. Such differences can be overcome by time and money -" He stopped, for she was looking at him with the same wondering interest, devoid of anger, with which he had seen her study Wilsey. "I express myself badly," he murmured.

Mrs. Wayne rose to her feet.

"The trouble isn't with your expression," she said.

"You mean that what I am trying to express is wrong?"

"It seems so to me."

"What is wrong about it?"

She seemed to think over the possibilities for an instant, and then she shook her head.

"I don't think I could make you understand," she answered. She said it very gently, but it was cruel, and he turned white under the pain, suffering all the more that she was so entirely without malice. She turned to her son. "I'm going, Pete. Don't you think you might as well come, too?"

Mathilde sprang up and caught Mrs. Wayne's hand.

"Oh, don't go!" she cried. "Don't take him away! You know they are trying to separate us. Oh, Mrs. Wayne, won't you take me in? Can't I stay with you while we are waiting?"

At this every one focused their eyes on Mrs. Wayne. Pete felt sorry for his mother, knowing how she hated to make a sudden decision, knowing how she hated to do anything disagreeable to those about her; but he never for an instant doubted what her decision would be. Therefore he could hardly believe his eyes when he

Alice Duer Miller

saw her shaking her head.

"I couldn't do that, my dear."

"Mother!"

"Of course you couldn't," said Mr. Lanley, blowing his nose immediately after under the tremendous emotion of finding that she was not an enemy, after all. Adelaide smiled to herself. She was thinking, "You could and would, if I hadn't put in that sting about his failures."

"Why can't you, Mother?" asked Pete.

"We'll talk that over at home."

"My dear boy," said Mr. Lanley, kindly, "no one over thirty would have to ask why."

"No parent likes to assist at the kidnapping of another parent's child," said Adelaide.

"Good Heavens! my mother has kidnapped so many children in her day!"

"From the wrong sort of home, I suppose," said Lanley, in explanation, to no one, perhaps, so much as to himself.

"Am I to infer that she thinks mine the right sort? How delightful!" said Adelaide.

"Mrs. Wayne, is it because I'm richer than Pete that you won't take me in?" asked Mathilde, visions of bestowing her wealth in charity flitting across her mind.

The other nodded. Wayne stared.

"Mother," he said, "you don't mean to say you are letting yourself be influenced by a taunt like that of Mrs. Farron's, which she didn't even believe herself?"

Mrs. Wayne was shocked.

"Oh, no; not that, Pete. It isn't that at all. But when a girl has been brought up -"

Wayne saw it all in an instant.

"Oh, yes, I see. We'll talk of that later."

But Adelaide had seen, too.

"No; do go on, Mrs. Wayne. You don't approve of the way my daughter has been brought up."

"I don't think she has been brought up to be a poor man's wife."

"No. I own I did not have that particular destiny in mind."

"And when I heard you assuming just now that every one was always concerned about money, and when I realized that the girl must have been brought up in that atmosphere and belief -"

"I see. You thought she was not quite the right wife for your son?"

"But I would try so hard," said Mathilde. "I would learn; I -"

"Mathilde," interrupted her mother, "when a lady tells you you are not good enough for her son, you must not protest."

"Come, come, Adelaide, there is no use in being disagreeable," said Mr. Lanley.

"Disagreeable!" returned his daughter. "Mrs. Wayne and I are entirely agreed. She thinks her son too good for my daughter, and I think my daughter too good for her son. Really, there seems nothing more to be said. Good-by, Mr. Wayne." She held out her long, white hand to him. Mrs. Wayne was trying to make her position clearer to Mathilde, but Pete thought this an undesirable moment for such an attempt.

Partly as an assertion of his rights, partly because she looked so young and helpless, he stopped and kissed her.

"I'll come and see you about half-past ten tomorrow morning," he said very clearly, so that every one could hear. Adelaide looked blank; she was thinking that on Pringle she could absolutely depend. Wayne saw his mother and Lanley bow to each other, and the next moment he had contrived to get her out of the house.

Mathilde rushed away to her own room, and Adelaide and her father were left alone. She turned to him with one of her rare caresses.

"Dear Papa," she said, "what a comfort you are to me! What should I do without you? You'll never desert me, will you?" And she put her head on his shoulder. He patted her with an absent-minded rhythm, and then he said, as if he were answering some secret train of thought:

"I don't see what else I could have done."

"You couldn't have done anything else," replied his daughter, still nestling against him. "But Mrs. Baxter had frightened me with her account of your sentimental admiration for Mrs. Wayne, and I thought you might want to make yourself agreeable to her at the expense of my poor child."

She felt his shoulder heave with a longer breath.

"I can't imagine putting anything before Mathilde's happiness," he said, and after a pause he added: "I really must go home. Mrs. Baxter will think me a neglectful host."

"Don't you want to bring her to dine here to-night? I'll try and get some one to meet her. Let me see. She thinks Mr. Wilsey -"

"Oh, I can't stand Wilsey," answered her father, crossly.

"Well, I'll think of some one to sacrifice on the altar of your friendship. I certainly don't want to dine alone with Mathilde. And, by the way, Papa, I haven't mentioned any of this to Vincent."

He thought it was admirable of her to bear her anxieties alone so as to spare her sick husband.

Alice Duer Miller

"Poor girl!" he said. "You've had a tot of trouble lately."

In the meantime Wayne and his mother walked slowly home.

"I suppose you're furious at me, Pete," she said.

"Not a bit," he answered. "For a moment, when I saw what you were going to say, I was terrified. But no amount of tact would have made Mrs. Farron feel differently, and I think they might as well know what we really think and feel. I was only sorry if it hurt Mathilde."

"Oh dear, it's so hard to be truthful!" exclaimed his mother. He laughed, for he wished she sometimes found it harder; and she went on:

"Poor little Mathilde! You know I wouldn't hurt her if I could help it. It's not her fault. But what a terrible system it is, and how money does blind people! They can't see you at all as you are, and yet if you had fifty thousand dollars a year, they'd be more aware of your good points than I am. They can't see that you have resolution and charm and a sense of honor. They don't see the person, they just see the lack of income."

Pete smiled.

"A person is all Mrs. Farron says she asks for her daughter."

"She does not know a person when she sees one."

"She knew one when she married Farron."

Mrs. Wayne sniffed.

"Perhaps he married her," she replied.

Her son thought this likely, but he did not answer, for she had given him an idea - to see Farron. Farron would at least understand the situation. His mother approved of the suggestion.

"Of course he's not Mathilde's father."

"He's not a snob."

They had reached the house, and Pete was fishing in his pocket for his keys.

"Do you think Mr. Lanley is a snob?" he asked.

As usual Mrs. Wayne evaded the direct answer.

"I got an unfavorable impression of him this afternoon."

"For failing to see that I was a king among men?"

"For backing up every stupid thing his daughter said."

"Loyalty is a fine quality."

"Justice is better," answered his mother.

"Oh, well, he's old," said Wayne, dismissing the whole subject.

They walked up their four flights in silence, and then Wayne remembered to ask something that had been in

Alice Duer Miller

his mind several times.

"By the way, Mother, how did you happen to come to the Farrons at all?"

She laughed rather self-consciously.

"I hoped perhaps Mr. Farron might be well enough to see me a moment about Marty. The truth is, Pete, Mr. Farron is the real person in that whole family."

That evening he wrote Farron a note, asking him to see him the next morning at half-past ten about "this trouble of which, of course, Mrs. Farron has told you." He added a request that he would tell Pringle of his intention in case he could give the interview, because Mrs. Farron had been quite frank in saying that she would give orders not to let him in.

Farron received this note with his breakfast. Adelaide was not there. He had had no hint from her of any crisis. He had not come down to dinner the evening before to meet Mrs. Baxter and the useful people asked to entertain her, but he had seen Mathilde's tear-stained face, and in a few minutes with his father-in-law had encountered one or two evident evasions. Only Adelaide had been unfathomable.

After he had read the letter and thought over the situation, he sent for Pringle, and gave orders that when Mr. Wayne came he would see him.

Pringle did not exactly make an objection, but stated a fact when he replied that Mrs. Farron had given orders that Mr. Wayne was not to be allowed to see Miss Severance.

"Exactly," said Farron. "Show him here." Here was his own study.

As it happened, Adelaide was sitting with him, making very good invalid's talk, when Pringle announced, "Mr. Wayne."

"Pringle, I told you -" Adelaide began, but her husband cut her short.

"He has an appointment with me, Adelaide."

"You don't understand, Vin. You mustn't see him."

Wayne was by this time in the room.

"But I wish to see him, my dear Adelaide, and," Farron added, "I wish to see him alone."

"No," she answered, with a good deal of excitement; "that you cannot. This is my affair, Vincent - the affair of my child."

He looked at her for a second, and then opening the door into his bedroom, he said to Wayne:

"Will you come in here?" The door was closed behind the two men.

Wayne was not a coward, although he had dreaded his interview with Adelaide; it was his very respect for Farron that kept him from feeling even nervous.

"Perhaps I ought not to have asked you to see me," he began.

"I'm very glad to see you," answered Farron. "Sit down, and tell me the story as you see it from the beginning."

It was a comfort to tell the story at last to an expert. Wayne, who had been trying for twenty-four hours to explain what underwriting meant, what were the responsibilities of brokers in such matters, what was the function of such a report as his, felt as if he had suddenly groped his way out of a fog as he talked, with hardly an interruption but a nod or a lightening eye from Farron. He spoke of Benson. "I know the man," said Farron; of Honaton, "He was in my office once." Wayne told how Mathilde, and then he himself, had tried to inform Mrs. Farron of the definiteness of their plans to be married.

"How long has this been going on?" Farron asked.

"At least ten days."

Farron nodded. Then Wayne told of the discovery of the proof at the printer's and his hurried meeting in the park to tell Mathilde. Here Farron stopped him suddenly.

"What was it kept you from going through with it just the same?"

"You're the first person who has asked me that," answered Pete.

"Perhaps you did not even think of such a thing?"

"No one could help thinking of it who saw her there -"

"And you didn't do it?"

"It wasn't consideration for her family that held me back."

"What was it?"

Pete found a moral scruple was a difficult motive to avow.

"It was Mathilde herself. That would not have been treating her as an equal."

"You intend always to treat her as an equal?"

Wayne was ashamed to find how difficult it was to answer truthfully. The tone of the question gave him no clue to the speaker's own thoughts.

"Yes, I do," he said; and then blurted out hastily, "Don't you believe in treating a woman as an equal?"

"I believe in treating her exactly as she wants to be treated."

"But every one wants to be treated as an equal, if they're any good." Farron smiled, showing those blue-white teeth for an instant, and Wayne, feeling he was not quite doing himself justice, added, "I call that just ordinary respect, you know, and I could not love any one I didn't respect. Could you?"

The question was, or Farron chose to consider it, a purely rhetorical one.

"I suppose," he observed, "that they are to be counted

the most fortunate who love and respect at the same time."

"Of course," said Wayne.

Farron nodded.

"And yet perhaps they miss a good deal."

"I don't know *what* they miss," answered Wayne, to whom the sentiment was as shocking as anything not understood can be.

"No; I'm sure you don't," answered his future step-father-in-law. "Go on with your story."

Wayne went on, but not as rapidly as he had expected. Farron kept him a long time on the interview of the afternoon before, and particularly on Mrs. Farron's part, just the point Wayne did not want to discuss for fear of betraying the bitterness he felt toward her. But again and again Farron made him quote her words wherever he could remember them; and then, as if this had not been clear enough, he asked:

"You think my wife has definitely made up her mind against the marriage?"

"Irrevocably."

"Irrevocably?" Farron questioned more as if it were the sound of the word than the meaning that he was doubting.

"Ah, you've been rather out of it lately, sir," said Wayne. "You haven't followed, perhaps, all that's been going on."

"Perhaps not."

Wayne felt he must be candid.

"If it is your idea that your wife's opposition could be changed, I'm afraid I must tell you, Mr. Farron -" He paused, meeting a quick, sudden look; then Farron turned his head, and stared, with folded arms, out of the window. Wayne had plenty of time to wonder what he was going to say. What he did say was surprising.

"I think you are an honest man, and I should be glad to have you working for me. I could make you one of my secretaries, with a salary of six thousand dollars."

In the shock Pete heard himself saying the first thing that came into his head:

"That's a large salary, sir."

"Some people would say large enough to marry on."

Wayne drew back.

"Don't you think you ought to consult Mrs. Farron before you offer it to me?" he asked hesitatingly.

"Don't carry honesty too far. No, I don't consult my wife about my office appointments."

"It isn't honesty; but I couldn't stand having you change your mind when -"

" When my wife tells me to? I promise you not to

do that."

Wayne found that the interview was over, although he had not been able to express his gratitude.

"I know what you are feeling," said Farron. "Good-by."

"I can't understand why you are doing it, Mr. Farron; but -"

"It needn't matter to you. Good-by."

With a sensation that in another instant he might be out of the house, Wayne metaphorically caught at the door-post.

"I must see Mathilde before I go," he said.

Farron shook his head.

"No, not to-day."

"She's terribly afraid I am going to be moved by insults to desert her," Wayne urged.

"I'll see she understands. I'll send for you in a day or two; then it will be all right." They shook hands. He was glad Farron showed him out through the corridor and not through the study, where, he knew, Mrs. Farron was still waiting like a fine, sleek cat at a rat-hole.

CHAPTER XV

During this interview Adelaide sat in her husband's study and waited. She looked back upon that other period of suspense - the hour when she had waited at the hospital during his operation - as a time of comparative peace. She had been able then, she remembered, to sit still, to pursue, if not a train of thought, at least a set of connected images; but now her whole spirit seemed to be seething with a sort of poison that made her muscles jerk and start and her mind dart and faint. Then she had foreseen loss through the fate common to humanity; now she foresaw it through the action of her own tyrannical contempt for anything that seemed to her weak.

She had never rebelled against coercion from Vincent. She had even loved it, but she had loved it when he had seemed to her a superior being; coercion from one who only yesterday had been under the dominion of nerves and nurses was intolerable to her. She was at heart a courtier, would do menial service to a king, and refuse common civility to an inferior. She knew how St. Christopher had felt at seeing his satanic captain tremble at the sign of the cross; and though, unlike the saint, she had no intention of setting out to discover the stronger lord, she knew that he might now any day appear.

Alice Duer Miller

From any one not an acknowledged superior that shut door was an insult to be avenged, and she sat and waited for the moment to arrive when she would most adequately avenge it. There was still something terrifying in the idea of going out to do battle with Vincent. Hitherto in their quarrels he had always been the aggressor, had always startled her out of an innocent calm by an accusation or complaint. But this, as she said to herself, was not a quarrel, but a readjustment, of which probably he was still unaware. She hoped he was. She hoped he would come in with his accustomed manner and say civilly, "Forgive me for shutting the door; but my reason was -"

And she would answer, "Really, I don't think we need trouble about your reasons, Vincent." She knew just the tone she would use, just the expression of a smile suppressed. Then his quick eyes would fasten themselves on her face, and perhaps at the first glance would read the story of his defeat. She knew her own glance would not waver.

At the end of half an hour she heard the low tones of conversation change to the brisk notes of leave-taking. Her heart began to beat with fear, but not the kind of fear that makes people run away; rather the kind that makes them abdicate all reason and fan their emotions into a sort of inspiring flame.

She heard the door open into the corridor, but even then Vincent did not immediately come. Miss Gregory had been waiting to say good-by to him. As a case he was finished. Adelaide heard her clear voice say gaily:

"Well, I'm off, Mr. Vincent."

They went back into the room and shut the door. Adelaide clenched her hands; these delays were hard to bear.

It was not a long delay, though in that next room a very human bond was about to be broken. Possibly if Vincent had done exactly what his impulses prompted, he would have taken Miss Gregory in his arms and kissed her. But instead he said quietly, for his manner had not much range:

"I shall miss you."

"It's time I went."

"To some case more interestingly dangerous?"

"Your case was dangerous enough for me," said the girl; and then for fear he might miss her meaning, "I never met any one like you, Mr. Farron."

"I've never been taken care of as you took care of me."

"I wish" - she looked straight up at him - "I could take care of you altogether."

"That," he answered, "would end in my taking care of you."

"And your hands are pretty full as it is?"

He nodded, and she went away without even shaking hands. She omitted her farewells to any other member of the family except Pringle, who, Farron heard, was congratulating her on her consideration for servants as he put her into her taxi.

Then he opened the door of his study, went to the chair he had risen from, and took up the paper at the paragraph at which he had dropped it. Adelaide's eyes followed him like search-lights.

"May I ask," she said with her edged voice, "if you have been disposing of my child's future in there without consulting me?"

If their places had been reversed, Adelaide would have raised her eyebrows and repeated, "Your child's future?" but Farron was more direct.

"I have been engaging Wayne as a secretary," he said, and, turning to the financial page, glanced down the quotations.

"Then you must dismiss him again."

"He will be a useful man to me," said Farron, as if she had not spoken. "I have needed some one whom I could depend on -"

"Vincent, it is absurd for you to pretend you don't know he wanted to marry Mathilde."

He did not raise his eyes.

"Yes," he said; "I remember you and I had some talk about it before my operation."

"Since then circumstances have arisen of which you know nothing - things I did not tell you."

"Do you think that was wise?"

With a sense that a rapid and resistless current was carrying them both to destruction she saw for the first time that he was as angry as she.

"I do not like your tone," she said.

"What's the matter with it?"

"It isn't polite; it isn't friendly."

"Why should it be?"

"Why? What a question! Love -"

"I doubt if it is any longer a question of love between you and me."

These words, which so exactly embodied her own idea, came to her as a shock, a brutal blow from him.

"Vincent!" she cried protestingly.

"I don't know what it is that has your attention now, what private anxieties that I am not privileged to share -"

"You have been ill."

"But not imbecile. Do you suppose I've missed one tone of your voice, or haven't understood what has been going on in your mind? Have you lived with me five years and think me a forgiving man -"

"May I ask what you have to forgive?"

"Do you suppose a pat to my pillow or an occasional

Alice Duer Miller

kind word takes the place to me of what our relation used to be?"

"You speak as if our relation was over."

"Have you been imagining I was going to come whining to you for a return of your love and respect? What nonsense! Love makes love, and indifference makes indifference."

"You expect me to say I am indifferent to you?"

"I care very little what you say. I judge your conduct."

She had an unerring instinct for what would wound him. If she had answered with conviction, "Yes, I am indifferent to you," there would have been enough temper and exaggeration in it for him to discount the whole statement. But to say, "No, I still love you, Vincent," in a tone that conceded the very utmost that she could, - namely, that she still loved him for the old, rather pitiful association, - that would be to inflict the most painful wound possible. And so that was what she said. She was prepared to have him take it up and cry: "You still love me? Do you mean as you love your Aunt Alberta?" and she, still trying to be just, would answer: "Oh, more than Aunt Alberta. Only, of course -"

The trouble was he did not make the right answer. When she said, "No, I still love you, Vincent," he answered:

"I cannot say the same."

It was one of those replies that change the face of the

world. It drove every other idea out of her head. She stared at him for an instant.

"Nobody," she answered, "need tell me such a thing as that twice." It was a fine phrase to cover a retreat; she left him and went to her own room. It no more occurred to her to ask whether he meant what he said than if she had been struck in the head she would have inquired if the blow was real.

She did not come down to lunch. Vincent and Mathilde ate alone. Mathilde, as she told Pete, had begun to understand her stepfather, but she had not progressed so far as to see in his silence anything but an unapproachable sternness. It never crossed her mind that this middle-aged man, who seemed to control his life so completely, was suffering far more than she, and she was suffering a good deal.

Pete had promised to come that morning, and she hadn't seen him yet. She supposed he had come, and that, though she had been on the lookout for him, she had missed him. She felt as if they were never going to see each other again. When she found she was to be alone at luncheon with Farron, she thought of appealing to him, but was restrained by two considerations. She was a kind person, and her mother had repeatedly impressed upon her how badly at present Mr. Farron supported any anxiety. More important than this, however, was her belief that he would never work at cross-purposes with his wife. What were she and Pete to do? She thought. Mrs. Wayne would not take her in, her mother would not let Pete come to the house, and they had no money.

Both cups of soup left the table almost untasted.

Alice Duer Miller

"I'm sorry Mama has one of her headaches," said Mathilde.

"Yes," said Farron. "You'd better take some of that chicken, Mathilde. It's very good."

She did not notice that the piece he had taken on his own plate was untouched.

"I'm not hungry," she answered.

"Anything wrong?"

She could not lie, and so she looked at him and smiled and answered:

"Nothing, as Mama would say, to trouble an invalid with."

She did not have a great success. In fact, his brows showed a slight disposition to contract, and after a moment of silence he said:

"Does your mother say that?"

"She's always trying to protect you nowadays, Mr. Farron."

"I saw your friend Pete Wayne this morning."

"You saw -" Surprise, excitement, alarm flooded her face with crimson. "Oh, why did *you* see him?"

"I saw him by appointment. He asked me to tell you - only, I'm afraid, other things put it out of my head - that he has accepted a job I offered him."

"O Mr. Farron, what kind of job?"

"Well, the kind of job that would enable two self-denying young people to marry, I think."

Not knowing how clearly all that she felt was written on her face Mathilde tried to put it all into words.

"How wonderful! how kind! But my mother -"

"I will arrange it with your mother."

"Have you known all along? Oh, why did you do this wonderful thing?"

"Because - perhaps you won't agree with me - I have taken rather a fancy to this young man. And I had other reasons."

Mathilde took her stepfather's hand as it lay upon the table.

"I've only just begun to understand you, Mr. Farron. To understand, I mean, what Mama means when she says you are the strongest, wisest person -"

He pretended to smile.

"When did your mother say that?"

"Oh, ages ago." She stopped, aware of a faint motion to withdraw on the part of the hand she held. "I suppose you want to go to her."

"No. The sort of headache she has is better left alone, I think, though you might stop as you go up."

"I will. When do you think I can see Pete?"

"I'd wait a day or two; but you might telephone him at once, if you like, and say - or do you know what to say?"

She laughed.

"It used to frighten me when you made fun of me like that; but now - It must be simply delirious to be able to make people as happy as you've just made us."

He smiled at her word.

"Other people's happiness is not exactly delirious," he said.

She was moving in the direction of the nearest telephone, but she said over her shoulder:

"Oh, well, I think you did pretty well for yourself when you chose Mama."

She left him sipping his black coffee; he took every drop of that.

When he had finished he did not go back to his study, but to the drawing-room, where he sat down in a large chair by the fire. He lit a cigar. It was a quiet hour in the house, and he might have been supposed to be a man entirely at peace.

Mr. Lanley, coming in about an hour later, certainly imagined he was rousing an invalid from a refreshing rest. He tried to retreat, but found Vincent's black eyes were on him.

"I'm sorry to disturb you," he said. "Just wanted to see Adelaide."

"Adelaide has a headache."

Life was taking so many wrong turnings that Mr. Lanley had grown apprehensive. He suddenly remembered how many headaches Adelaide had had just before he knew of her troubles with Severance.

"A headache?" he said nervously.

"Nothing serious." Vincent looked more closely at his father-in-law. "You yourself don't look just the thing, sir."

Mr. Lanley sat down more limply than was his custom.

"I'm getting to an age," he said, "when I can't stand scenes. We had something of a scene here yesterday afternoon. God bless my soul! though, I believe Adelaide told me not to mention it to you."

"Adelaide is very considerate," replied her husband. His extreme susceptibility to sorrow made Mr. Lanley notice a tone which ordinarily would have escaped him, and he looked up so sharply that Farron was forced to add quickly: "But you haven't made a break. I know about what took place."

The egotism of suffering, the distorted vision of a sleepless night, made Mr. Lanley blurt out suddenly:

"I want to ask you, Vincent, do you think I could have done anything different?"

Alice Duer Miller

Now, none of the accounts which Farron had received had made any mention of Mr. Lanley's part in the proceedings at all, and so he paused a moment, and in that pause Mr. Lanley went on:

"It's a difficult position - before a boy's mother. There isn't anything against him, of course. One's reasons for not wanting the marriage do sound a little snobbish when one says them - right out. In fact, I suppose they are snobbish. Do you find it hard to get away from early prejudices, Vincent? I do. I think Adelaide is quite right; and yet the boy is a nice boy. What do you think of him?"

"I have taken him into my office."

Mr. Lanley was startled by a courage so far beyond his own.

"But," he asked, "did you consult Adelaide?"

Farron shook his head.

"But, Vincent, was that quite loyal?"

A change in Farron's expression made Mr. Lanley turn his head, and he saw that Adelaide had come into the room. Her appearance bore out the legend of her headache: she looked like a garden after an early frost. But perhaps the most terrifying thing about her aspect was her complete indifference to it. A recollection suddenly came to Mr. Lanley of a railway accident that he and Adelaide had been in. He had seen her stepping toward him through the debris, buttoning her gloves. She was far beyond such considerations now.

She had come to put her very life to the test. There was one hope, there was one way in which Vincent could rehabilitate himself, and that was by showing himself victor in the hardest of all struggles, the personal struggle with her. That would be hard, because she would make it so, if she perished in the attempt.

The crisis came in the first meeting of their eyes. If his glance had said: "My poor dear, you're tired. Rest. All will be well," his cause would have been lost. But his glance said nothing, only studied her coolly, and she began to speak.

"Oh, Papa, Vincent does not consider such minor points as loyalty to me." Her voice and manner left Mr. Lanley in no doubt that if he stayed an instant he would witness a domestic quarrel. The idea shocked him unspeakably. That these two reserved and dignified people should quarrel at all was bad enough, but that they should have reached a point where they were indifferent to the presence of a third person was terrible. He got himself out of the room without ceremony, but not before he saw Vincent rise and heard the first words of his sentence:

"And what right have you to speak of loyalty?" Here, fortunately, Lanley shut the door behind him, for Vincent's next words would have shocked him still more: "A prostitute would have stuck better to a man when he was ill."

But Adelaide was now in good fighting trim. She laughed out loud.

"Really, Vincent," she said, "your language! You must make your complaint against me a little more definite."

"Not much; and give you a chance to get up a little rational explanation. Besides, we neither of us need explanations. We know what has been happening."

"You mean you really doubt my feeling for you? No, Vincent, I still love you," and her voice had a flute-like quality which, though it was without a trace of conviction, very few people who had ever heard it had resisted.

"I am aware of that," said Vincent quietly.

She looked beautifully dazed.

"Yet this morning you spoke - as if -"

"But what is love such as yours worth? A man must be on the crest of the wave to keep it; otherwise it changes automatically into contempt. I don't care about it, Adelaide. I can't use it in a life like mine."

She looked at him, and a dreamlike state began to come over her. She simply couldn't believe in the state of mind of those sick-room days; she could never really, she thought, have been less passionately admiring than she was at that minute, yet the half-recollection confused her and kept her silent.

"Perhaps it's vanity on my part," he said, "but contempt like yours is something I could never forgive."

"You would forgive me anything if you loved me." Her tone was noble and sincere.

"Perhaps."

"You mean you don't?"

"Adelaide, there are times when a person chooses between loving and being loved."

The sentence made her feel sick with fear, but she asked:

"Tell me just what you mean."

"Perhaps I could keep on loving you if I shut my eyes to the kind of person you are; but if I did that, I could not hold you an instant."

She stared at him as fascinated as a bird by a snake. This, it seemed to her, was the truth, the final summing up of their relation. She had lost him, and yet she was eternally his.

As she looked at him she became aware that he was growing slowly pale. He was standing, and he put his hand out to the mantelpiece to steady himself. She thought he was going to faint.

"Vincent," she said, "let me help you to the sofa."

She wanted now to see him falter, to feel his hand on her shoulder, anything for a closer touch with him. For half a minute, perhaps, they remained motionless, and then the color began to come back into his face.

He smiled bitterly.

"They tell me you are such a good sick nurse, Mrs. Farron," he said, "so considerate to the weak. But I don't need your help, thank you."

Alice Duer Miller

She covered her face with her hands. He seemed to her stronger and more cruel than anything she had imagined. In a minute he left her alone.

CHAPTER XVI

Farron cared, perhaps, no more for appearances than Adelaide did, but his habitual manner was much better adapted to concealment. In him the fluctuations between the deepest depression and the highest elation were accompanied by such slight variations of look and tone that they escaped almost every one but Adelaide herself. He came down to dinner that evening, and while Adelaide sat in silence, with her elbows on the table and her long fingers clasping and unclasping themselves in a sort of rhythmic desperation, conversation went on pleasantly enough between Mathilde and Vincent. This was facilitated by the fact that Mathilde had now transferred to Vincent the flattering affection which she used to give to her grandfather. She agreed with, wondered at, and drank in every word.

Naturally, Mathilde attributed her mother's distress to the crisis in her own love-affairs. She had had no word with her as to Wayne's new position, and it came to her in a flash that it would be daring, but wise, to take the matter up in the presence of her stepfather. So, as soon as they were in the drawing-room, and Farron had opened the evening paper, and his wife, with a wild decision, had opened a book, Mathilde ruthlessly interrupted them both, recalling them from what appeared to be the depths of absorptions in their

Alice Duer Miller

respective pages by saying:

"Mr. Farron, did you tell Mama what you had done about Pete?"

Farron raised his eyes and said:

"Yes."

"And what did she say?"

"What is there for me to say?" answered Adelaide in the terrible, crisp voice that Mathilde hated.

There was a pause. To Mathilde it seemed extraordinary the way older people sometimes stalled and shifted about perfectly obvious issues; but, wishing to be patient, she explained:

"Don't you see it makes some difference in our situation?"

"The greatest, I should think," said Adelaide, and just hinted that she might go back to her book at any instant.

"But don't you think -" Mathilde began again, when Farron interrupted her almost sharply.

"Mathilde," he said, "there's a well-known business axiom, not to try to get things on paper too early."

She bent her head a trifle on one side in the way a puppy will when an unusual strain is being put upon its faculties. It seemed to her curious, but she saw she was being advised to drop the subject. Suddenly Adelaide sprang to her feet and said she was going to bed.

"I hope your headache will be better, Mama," Mathilde hazarded; but Adelaide went without answering. Mathilde looked at Mr. Farron.

"You haven't learned to wait," he said.

"It's so hard to wait when you are on bad terms with people you love!"

She was surprised that he smiled - a smile that conveyed more pain than amusement.

"It is hard," he said.

This closed the evening. The next morning Vincent went down-town. He went about half-past ten. Adelaide, breakfasting in her room and dressing at her leisure, did not appear until after eleven, and then discovered for the first time that her husband had gone. She was angry at Mathilde, who had breakfasted with him, at Pringle, for not telling her what was happening.

"You shouldn't have let him go, Mathilde," she said. "You are old enough to have some judgment in such matters. He is not strong enough. He almost fainted yesterday."

"But, Mama," protested the girl, "I could not stop Mr. Farron. I don't think even you could have if he'd made up his mind."

"Tell Pringle to order the motor at once," was her mother's answer.

Her distraction at her husband's imprudence touched Mathilde so that she forgot everything else between them.

"O Mama," she said, "I'm so sorry you're worried! I'm sorry I'm one of your worries; but don't you see I love Pete just as you do Mr. Farron?"

"God help you, then!" said Adelaide, quickly, and went to her room to put on with a haste none the less meticulous her small velvet hat, her veil, her spotless, pale gloves, her muff, and warm coat.

She drove to Vincent's office. It was not really care for his health that drove her, but the restlessness of despair; she had reached a point where she was more wretched away from him than with him.

The office was high in a gigantic building. Every one knew her by sight, the giant at the door and the men in the elevators. Once in the office itself, a junior partner hurried to her side.

"So glad to see Vincent back again," he said, proud of the fact that he called his present partner and late employer by his first name. "You want to see him?" There was a short hesitation. "He left word not to be disturbed -"

"Who is there?" Adelaide asked.

"Dr. Parret."

"He's not been taken ill?"

He tried to reassure her, but Adelaide, without waiting

or listening, moved at once to Vincent's door and opened it. As she did so she heard, him laughing and then she saw that he was laughing at the words of the handsomest woman she had ever seen. A great many people had this first impression of Lily Parret. Lily was standing on the opposite side of the table from him, leaning with both palms flat on the polished wood, telling him some continued narrative that made her blue eyes shine and her dimples deepen.

Adelaide was not temperamentally jealous. She did not, like Vincent, hate and fear any person or thing or idea that drew his attention away; on the contrary, she wanted him to give his full attention to anything that would make for his power and success. She was not jealous, but it did cross her mind that she was looking now at her successor.

They stopped laughing as she entered, and Vincent said:

"Thank you, Dr. Parret, you have given me just what I wanted."

"Marty would just as lief as not stick a knife in me if he knew," said Lily, not as if she were afraid, but as if this was one of the normal risks of her profession. She turned to Adelaide, "O Mrs. Farron, I've heard of you from Pete Wayne. Isn't he perfectly delightful? But, then, he ought to be with such a mother."

Adelaide had a very useful smile, which could maintain a long, but somewhat meaningless, brilliance. She employed it now, and it lasted until Lily had gone.

"That's a very remarkable girl," said Farron, remembrances of smiles still on his lips.

"Does she think every one perfect?"

"Almost every one; that's how she keeps going at such a rate."

"How long have you known her?"

"About ten minutes. Pete got her here. She knew something about Marty that I needed." He spoke as if he was really interested in the business before him; he did not betray by so much as a glance the recognition that they were alone, though she was calling his attention to the fact by every line of her figure and expression of her face. She saw his hand move on his desk. Was it coming to hers? He rang a bell. "Is Burke in the outer office? Send him in."

Adelaide's heart began to beat as Marty, in his working-clothes, entered. He was more suppressed and more sulky than she had yet seen him.

"I've been trying to see you, Mr. Farron," he began; but Vincent cut in:

"One moment, Burke. I have something to say to you. That bout you said you had with O'Hallohan -"

"Well, what of it?" answered Marty, suddenly raising his voice.

"He knocked you out."

"Who says so?" roared Burke.

"He knocked you out," repeated Vincent.

"Who says so?" Burke roared again, and somehow there was less confidence in the same volume of sound.

"Well, not O'Hallohan; He stayed bought. But I have it straight. No, I'm not trying to draw you out on a guess. I don't play that kind of game. If I tell you I know if for a fact, I do."

"Well, and what of it?" said Marty.

"Just this. I wouldn't dismiss a man for getting knocked out by a bigger man -"

"He ain't bigger."

"By a better fighter, then; but I doubt whether or not I want a foreman who has to resort to that kind of thing - to buying off the man who licked -"

"I didn't *buy* him off," said Burke, as if he knew the distinction, even in his own mind, was a fine one.

"Oh, yes, you did," answered Farron. And getting up, with his hands in his pockets, he added, "I'm afraid your usefulness to me is over, Burke."

"The hell it is!"

"My wife is here, Marty," said Farron, very pleasantly. "But this story isn't the only thing I have against you. My friend Mrs. Wayne tells me you are exerting a bad influence over a fellow whose marriage she wants to get annulled."

"Oh, let 'em get it annulled!" shouted Marty on a high and rising key. "What do I care? I'll do anything to oblige if I'm asked right; but when Mrs. Wayne and that gang come around bullying me, I won't do a thing for them. But, if you ask me to, Mr. Farron, why, I'm glad to oblige you."

"Thank you, Marty," returned his employer, cordially. "If you arrange that for me, I must own it would make me feel differently. I tell you," he added, as one who suggests an honorable compromise, "you get that settled up, you get that marriage annulled - that is, if you think you can -"

"Sure I can," Burke replied, swaying his body about from the waist up, as if to indicate the ease with which it could be accomplished.

"Well, when that's done, come back, and we'll talk over the other matter. Perhaps, after all - well, we'll talk it over."

Burke walked to the door with his usual conquering step, but there turned.

"Say," he said, "that story about the fight -" He looked at Adelaide. "Ladies don't always understand these matters. Tell her, will you, that it's done in some first-class fights?"

"I'll explain," answered Vincent.

"And there ain't any use in the story's getting about," Burke added.

"It won't, " said Vincent. On which assurance Marty

went away and left the husband and wife alone.

Adelaide got up and went to the window and looked out toward the Palisades. Marty Burke had been a symbol that enabled her to recall some of her former attitudes of mind. She remembered that dinner where she had pitted him against her husband. She felt deeply humiliated in her own sight and in Vincent's, for she was now ready to believe that he had read her mind from the beginning. It seemed to her as if she had been mad, and in that madness had thrown away the only thing in the world she would ever value. The thought of acknowledging her fault was not repugnant to her; she had no special objection to groveling, but she knew it would do no good, Vincent, though not ungenerous, saw clearly; and he had summed up the situation in that terrible phrase about choosing between loving and being loved. "I suppose I shouldn't respect him much if he did forgive me," she thought; and suddenly she felt his arms about her; he snatched her to him, turned her face to his, calling her by strange, unpremeditated terms of endearment. Beyond these, no words at all were exchanged between them; they were undesired. Adelaide did not know whether it were servile or superb to care little about knowing his opinion and intentions in regard to her. All that she cared about was that in her eyes he was once more supreme and that his arms were about her. Words, she knew, would have been her enemies, and she did not make use of them.

When they went out, they passed Wayne in the outer office.

"Come to dinner to-night, Pete," said Farron, and added, turning to his wife, "That's all right, isn't it, Adelaide?"

Alice Duer Miller

She indicated that it was perfect, like everything he did.

Wayne looked at his future mother-in-law in surprise. His pride had been unforgetably stung by some of her sentences, but he could have forgiven those more easily than the easy smile with which she now nodded at her husband's invitation, as if a pleasant intention on her part could wipe out everything that had gone before. That, it seemed to him, was the very essence of insolence.

Appreciating that some sort of doubt was disturbing him, Adelaide said most graciously:

"Yes, you really must come, Mr. Wayne."

At this moment Farron's own stenographer, Chandler, approached him with an unsigned letter in his hand.

Chandler took the routine of the office more seriously than Farron did, and acquired thereby a certain power over his employer. He had something of the attitude of a child's nurse, who, knowing that her charge has almost passed beyond her care, recognizes that she has no authority except that bestowed by devotion.

"I think you meant to sign this letter, Mr. Farron," he said, just as a nurse might say before strangers, "You weren't going to the party without washing your hands?"

"Oh." Farron fished in his waistcoat for his pen, and while he was writing, and Chandler just keeping an eye on him to see that it was done right, Adelaide said:

"And how is Mrs. Chandler?"

Chandler's face lit up as he received the letter back.

"Oh, much better, thank you, Mrs. Farron - out of all danger."

Wayne saw, what Chandler did not, that Adelaide had never even heard of Mrs. Chandler's ill health; but she murmured as she turned away:

"I'm so glad. You must have been very anxious."

When they were gone, Wayne and Chandler were left a minute alone.

"What a personality!" Chandler exclaimed. "Imagine her remembering my troubles, when you think what she has had to worry about! A remarkable couple, Mr. Wayne. I have been up to the house a number of times since Mr. Farron's illness, and she is always there, so brave, so attentive. A queenly woman, and," he added, as if the two did not always go together, "a good wife."

Wayne could think of no answer to this eulogy, and as they stood in silence the office door opened and Mr. Lanley came in. He nodded to each of the two, and moved to Vincent's room.

"Mr. Farron has just gone," said Chandler, firmly. He could not bear to have people running in and out of Farron's room.

"Gone?" said Lanley, as if it were somebody's fault.

"Mrs. Farron came down for him in the motor. He

Alice Duer Miller

appeared to stand his first day very well."

Mr. Lanley glanced quickly from one to the other. This did not sound as if any final break had occurred between the Farrons, yet on this subject he could hardly question his son-in-law's secretaries. He made one further effort.

"I suppose Mr. Farron thought he was good for a whole day's work."

Chandler smiled.

"Mr. Farron, like all wise men, sir, does what his wife tells him." And then, as he loved his own work far more than conversation, Chandler hurried back to his desk.

"I understand," said Lanley to Wayne, "that you are here regularly now."

"Yes."

"Like your work?" Lanley was obviously delaying, hoping that some information would turn up unexpectedly.

"Very much."

"Humph! What does your mother think about it?"

"About my new job?" Wayne smiled. "You know those aren't the kind of facts - jobs and salaries - that my mother scrutinizes very closely."

Lanley stared at him with brows slightly contracted.

"What does she scrutinize?" he asked.

"Oh, motives - spiritual things."

"I see." Mr. Lanley couldn't go a step further, couldn't take this young man into his confidence an inch further. He stuck his stick into his overcoat-pocket so that it stood upright, and wheeled sharply.

"Good-by," he said, and added at the door, "I suppose you think this makes a difference in your prospects."

"Mrs. Farron has asked me to come to dinner to-night."

Lanley wheeled back again.

"What?" he said

"Yes, she almost urged me, though I didn't need urging."

Lanley didn't answer, but presently went out in silence. He was experiencing the extreme loneliness that follows being more royalist than the king.

CHAPTER XVII

On Mondays and Thursdays, the only days Mr. Lanley went down-town, he expected to have the corner table at the restaurant where he always lunched and where, on leaving Farron's office, he went. He had barely finished ordering luncheon - oyster stew, cold tongue, salad, and a bottle of Rhine wine - when, looking up, he saw Wilsey was approaching him, beaming.

"Haryer, Wilsey?" he said, without cordiality.

Wilsey, it fortunately appeared, had already had his midday meal, and had only a moment or two to give to sociability.

"Haven't seen you since that delightful evening," he murmured. "I hope Mrs. Baxter got my card." He mentioned his card as if it had been a gift, not munificent, but not negligible, either.

"Suppose she got it if you left it," said Mr. Lanley, who had heard her comment on it. "My man's pretty good at that sort of thing."

"Ah, how rare they are getting!" said Wilsey, with a sigh - "good servants. Upon my word, Lanley, I'm almost ready to go."

"Because you can't get good servants?" said his friend, who was drumming on the table and looking blankly about.

"Because all the old order is passing, all the standards and backgrounds that I value. I don't think I'm a snob -"

"Of course you're a snob, Wilsey."

Mr. Wilsey smiled temperately.

"What do you mean by the word?"

It was a question about which Lanley had been thinking, and he answered:

"I mean a person who values himself for qualities that have no moral, financial, or intellectual value whatsoever. You, for instance, Wilsey, value yourself not because you are a pretty good lawyer, but because your great-grandfather signed the Declaration."

A shade of slight embarrassment crossed the lawyer's face.

"I own," he said, "that I value birth, but so do you, Lanley. You attach importance to being a New York Lanley."

"I do," answered Lanley; "but I have sense enough to be ashamed of doing so. You're proud of being proud of your old Signer."

"As a matter of fact," Mr. Wilsey remarked slowly, "Josiah Wilsey did not sign the Declaration."

"What!" cried Lanley. "You've always told me he did."

Wilsey shook his head gently, as one who went about correcting errors.

"No. What I said was that I feel no moral doubt he would have signed it if an attack of illness -"

Lanley gave a short roar.

"That's just like *you*, Wilsey. You wouldn't have signed it, either. You would have said that while in cordial sympathy with the ideas set forth, you would not care to put your name to a document that might give pain to a monarch who, though not as liberal as some of us could wish, was yet -"

"As a matter of fact," Wilsey began again even more coldly, "I should have signed -"

"Oh, you think so now. A hundred years from now you'd sign a petition for the eight-hour law."

"Never!" said Wilsey, raising his hand. "I should never put my name to a document -" He stopped at another roar from his friend, and never took the sentence up again, but indicated with a gesture that only legal minds were worth arguing with on points of this sort.

When he had gone, Lanley dipped the spoon in his oyster stew with not a little pleasure. Nothing, apparently, could have raised his spirits more than the knowledge that old Josiah Wilsey had not signed the Declaration. He actually chuckled a little. "So like Wilsey himself," he thought. "No moral courage; calls it conservatism." Then his joy abated. Just so, he thought, must he himself appear to Mrs. Wayne. Yet his self-respect insisted that his case was different. Loyalty had been responsible not for his conservatism, but for the pig-headedness with which he had acted upon it. He would have asked nothing better than to profess himself open-minded to Mrs. Wayne's views, only he could not desert Adelaide in the moment of her struggle for beliefs in which he himself had brought her up. And now she had deserted him. He alone was left to flaunt a banner the motto of which he didn't wholly believe, while Adelaide, at a word from Vincent, had gone over to the other side. And no one knew what his loyalty had cost him. Long ago, in his first year at college, he had flunked the examination of the professor whom he reverenced above all others. No one had cared, no one had long remembered, except Lanley himself, and he had remembered because some one had told him what the professor said on reading his paper. It was nothing but, "I had supposed Lanley was intelligent." Never again had he had that professor's attention for a single instant. This, it seemed to him, was about to happen to him again, now when it was too late in his life to do anything but despair.

He called the waiter, paid his bill and tip, - he was an extremely liberal tipper; "it's expected of us," he used to say, meaning that it was expected of people like the New York Lanleys, - and went away.

In old times he had been an inventor of many clever tricks for getting up-town by unpopular elevated trains and horse-cars that avoided the crowd, but the subway was a great leveler, and he knew no magic except to take a local in rush hours. At three o'clock, however, even this was not necessary. He took an express, and got off at the Grand Central, turned up Park Avenue,

Alice Duer Miller

and then east. He had just found out that he was going to visit Mrs. Wayne.

He read the names in the vestibule, never doubting that Dr. Parret was a masculine practitioner, and hesitated at the name of Wayne. He thought he ought to ring the bell, but he wanted to go straight up. Some one had left the front door unlatched. He pushed it open and began the steep ascent.

She came to the door of the flat herself. She had a funny little gray shawl about her shoulders and a pen in her hand. She tried to make her voice sound very cordial as she greeted him, but he thought he caught something that sounded as if, while perfectly well disposed to him, she couldn't for the life of her imagine why he had come.

"Come in," she said, "though I'm afraid it's a little cold in here. Our janitor -"

"Let me light your fire for you," he answered, and extracting a parlor-match from his pocket, - safety-matches were his bugbear, - he stooped, and put the flame to the fire. As he did so he understood that it was not the mere forgetfulness of a servant that had left it unlighted, but probably a deliberate economy, and he rose crimson and unhappy.

It took him some time to recover, and during the entire time she sat in her gray shawl, looking very amiable, but plainly unable to think of anything to say.

"I saw your son in Farron's office to-day."

"Mr. Farron has been so kind, so wonderfully kind!"

Only a guilty conscience could have found reproach in this statement, and Lanley said:

"And I hear he is dining at my daughter's this evening."

Mrs. Wayne had had a telephone message to that effect.

"I wondered, if you were alone -" Lanley hesitated. He had of course been going to ask her to come and dine with him, but a better inspiration came to him. "I wondered if you would ask me to dine with you."

"Oh, I'm so sorry," said Mrs. Wayne, "but I can't. I have a boy coming. He's studying for the ministry, the most interesting person. He had not been sober for three years when I took hold of him, and now he hasn't touched a drop for two."

He sighed. She said she was sorry, but he could see plainly enough that any reformed, or even more any unreformed, drunkard would always far surpass him in ability to command her interest. He did not belong to a generation that cleared things up with words; he would have thought it impertinent, almost ungentlemanly, to probe her attitude of mind about the scene at Adelaide's; and he would have considered himself unmanly to make any plea to her on the ground of his own suffering. One simply supported such things as best one could; it was expected of one, like tipping waiters. He had neither the vocabulary nor the habit of mind that made an impersonal exposition of an emotional difficulty possible; but even had he possessed these powers he would have retained his tradition against using them. Perhaps, if she had been his sister or his wife, he might have admitted that he had had a hard day or that every one had moments of depression; but that was not the way to talk in a lady's drawing-room. In the silence he saw her eyes steal longingly to her writing-table, deeply and hopelessly littered with papers and open books.

"I'm afraid I'm detaining you," he said. The visit had been a failure.

"Oh, not at all," she replied, and then added in a tone of more sincerity: "I do have the most terrible time with my check-book. And," she added, as one confessing to an absurdly romantic ideal, "I was trying to balance it."

"You should not be troubled with such things," said Mr. Lanley, thinking how long it was since any one but a secretary had balanced his books.

Pete, it appeared, usually did attend to his mother's checks, but of late she had not liked to bother him, and that was just the moment the bank had chosen to notify her that she had overdrawn. "I don't see how I can be," she said, too hopeless to deny it.

"If you would allow me," said Mr. Lanley. "I am an excellent bookkeeper."

"Oh, I shouldn't like to trouble you," said Mrs. Wayne, but she made it clear she would like it above everything; so Lanley put on his spectacles, drew up his chair, and squared his elbows to the job.

"It hasn't been balanced since - dear me! not since October," he said.

"I know; but I draw such small checks."

"But you draw a good many."

She had risen, and was standing before the fire, with her hands behind her back. Her shawl had slipped off, and she looked, in her short walking-skirt, rather like a school-girl being reprimanded for a poor exercise. She felt so when, looking up at her over his spectacles, he observed severely:

"You really must be more careful about carrying forward. Twice you have carried forward an amount from two pages back instead of -"

"That's always the way," she interrupted. "Whenever people look at my check-book they take so long scolding me about the way I do it that there's no time left for putting it right."

"I won't say another word," returned Lanley; "only it would really help you -"

"I don't want any one to do it who says my sevens are like fours," she went on. Lanley compressed his lips slightly, but contented himself by merely lengthening the tail of a seven. He said nothing more, but every time he found an error he gave a little shake of his head that went through her like a knife.

The task was a long one. The light of the winter afternoon faded, and she lit the lamps before he finished. At first he had tried not to be aware of revelations that the book made; but as he went on and he found he was obliged now and then to question her about payments and receipts, he saw that she was so

Alice Duer Miller

utterly without any sense of privacy in the matter that his own decreased.

He had never thought of her as being particularly poor, not at least in the sense of worrying over every bill, but now when he saw the small margin between the amounts paid in and the amounts paid out, when he noticed how large a proportion of what she had she spent in free gifts and not in living expenses, he found himself facing something he could not tolerate. He put his pen down carefully in the crease of the book, and rose to his feet.

"Mrs. Wayne," he said, "I must tell you something."

"You're going to say, after all, that my sevens are like fours."

"I'm going to say something worse - more inexcusable. I'm going to tell you how much I want you to honor me by becoming my wife."

She pronounced only one syllable. She said, "*Oh!*" as crowds say it when a rocket goes off.

"I suppose you think it ridiculous in a man of my age to speak of love, but it's not ridiculous, by Heaven! It's tragic. I shouldn't have presumed, though, to mention the subject to you, only it is intolerable to me to think of your lacking anything when I have so much. I can't explain why this knowledge gave me courage. I know that you care nothing for luxuries and money, less than any one I know; but the fact that you haven't everything that you ought to have makes me suffer so much that I hope you will at least listen to me."

"But you know it doesn't make me suffer a bit," said Mrs. Wayne.

"To know you at all has been such a happiness that I am shocked at my own presumption in asking for your companionship for the rest of my life, and if in addition to that I could take care of you, share with you -"

No one ever presented a proposition to Mrs. Wayne without finding her willing to consider it, an open-mindedness that often led her into the consideration of absurdities. And now the sacred cupidity of the reformer did for an instant leap up within her. All the distressed persons, all the tottering causes in which she was interested, seemed to parade before her eyes. Then, too, the childish streak in her character made her remember how amusing it would be to be Adelaide Farron's mother-in-law, and Peter's grandmother by marriage. Nor was she at all indifferent to the flattery of the offer or the touching reserves of her suitor's nature.

"I should think you would be so lonely!" he said gently.

She nodded.

"I am often. I miss not having any one to talk to over the little things that" - she laughed - "I probably wouldn't talk over if I had some one. But even with Pete I am lonely. I want to be first with some one again."

"You will always be first with me."

"Even if I don't marry you?"

"Whatever you do."

Like the veriest coquette, she instantly decided to take all and give nothing - to take his interest, his devotion, his loyalty, all of the first degree, and give him in return a divided interest, a loyalty too much infected by humor to be complete, and a devotion in which several causes and Pete took precedence. She did not do this in ignorance. On the contrary, she knew just how it would be; that he would wait and she be late, that he would adjust himself and she remain unchanged, that he would give and give and she would never remember that it would be kind some day to ask. Yet it did not seem to her an unfair bargain, and perhaps she was right.

"I couldn't marry you," she said. "I couldn't change. All your pretty things and the way you live - it would be like a cage to me. I like my life the way it is; but yours -"

"Do you think I would ask Wilsey to dinner every night or try to mold you to be like Mrs. Baxter?"

She laughed.

"You'd have a hard time. I never could have married again. I'd make you a poor wife, but I'm a wonderful friend."

"Your friendship would be more happiness than I had any right to hope for," and then he added in a less satisfied tone: "But friendship is so uncertain. You don't make any announcements to your friends or vows to each other, unless you're at an age when you cut your initials in the bark of a tree. That's what I'd like to do. I suppose you think I'm an old fool."

"Two of us," said Mrs. Wayne, and wiped her eyes. She cried easily, and had never felt the least shame about it.

It was a strange compact - strange at least for her, considering that only a few hours before she had thought of him as a friendly, but narrow-minded, old stranger. Something weak and malleable in her nature made her enter lightly into the compact, although all the time she knew that something more deeply serious and responsible would never allow her to break it. A faint regret for even an atom of lost freedom, a vein of caution and candor, made her say:

"I'm so afraid you'll find me unsatisfactory. Every one has, even Pete."

"I think I shall ask less than any one," he returned.

The answer pleased her strangely.

Presently a ring came at the bell - a telegram. The expected guest was detained at the seminary. Lanley watched with agonized attention. She appeared to be delighted.

"Now you'll stay to dine," she said. "I can't remember what there is for dinner."

"Now, that's not friendly at the start," said he, "to think I care so much."

Alice Duer Miller

"Well, you're not like a theological student."

"A good deal better, probably," answered Lanley, with a gruffness that only partly hid his happiness. There was no real cloud in his sky. If Mrs. Wayne had accepted his offer of marriage, by this time he would have begun to think of the horror of telling Adelaide and Mathilde and his own servants. Now he thought of nothing but the agreeable evening before him, one of many.

When Pete came in to dress, Lanley was just in the act of drawing the last neat double lines for his balance. He had been delayed by the fact that Mrs. Wayne had been talking to him almost continuously since his return to figuring. She was in high spirits, for even saints are stimulated by a respectful adoration.

CHAPTER XVIII

Recognizing the neat back of Mr. Lanley's gray head, Pete's first idea was that he must have come to induce Mrs. Wayne to conspire with him against the marriage; but he abandoned this notion on seeing his occupation.

"Hullo, Mr. Lanley," he said, stooping to kiss his mother with the casual affection of the domesticated male. "You have my job."

"It is a great pleasure to be of any service," said Mr. Lanley.

"It was in a terrible state, it seems, Pete," said his mother.

"She makes her fours just like sevens, doesn't she?" observed Pete.

"I did not notice the similarity," replied Mr. Lanley. He glanced at Mrs. Wayne, however, and enjoyed his denial almost as much as he had enjoyed the discovery that the Wilsey ancestor had not been a Signer. He felt that somehow, owing to his late-nineteenth-century tact, the breach between him and Pete had been healed.

"Mr. Lanley is going to stay and dine with me," said Mrs. Wayne.

Alice Duer Miller

Pete looked a little grave, but his next sentence explained the cause of his anxiety.

"Wouldn't you like me to go out and get something to eat, Mother?"

"No, no," answered his mother, firmly. "This time there really is something in the house quite good. I don't remember what it is."

And then Pete, who felt he had done his duty, went off to dress. Soon, however, his voice called from an adjoining room.

"Hasn't that woman sent back any of my collars, Mother dear?"

"O Pete, her daughter got out of the reformatory only yesterday," Mrs. Wayne replied. Lanley saw that the Wayne housekeeping was immensely complicated by crime. "I believe I am the only person in your employ not a criminal," he said, closing the books. "These balance now."

"Have I anything left?"

"Only about a hundred and fifty."

She brightened at this.

"Oh, come," she said, "that's not so bad. I couldn't have been so terribly overdrawn, after all."

"You ought not to overdraw at all," said Mr. Lanley, severely. "It's not fair to the bank."

"Well, I never mean to," she replied, as if no one could ask more than that.

Presently she left him to go and dress for dinner. He felt extraordinarily at home, left alone like this among her belongings. He wandered about looking at the photographs - photographs of Pete as a child, a photograph of an old white house with wisteria-vines on it; a picture of her looking very much as she did now, with Pete as a little boy, in a sailor suit, leaning against her; and then a little photograph of her as a girl not much older than Mathilde, he thought - a girl who looked a little frightened and awkward, as girls so often looked, and yet to whom the French photographer - for it was taken in the Place de la Madeleine - had somehow contrived to give a Parisian air. He had never thought of her in Paris. He took the picture up; it was dated May, 1884. He thought back carefully. Yes, he had been in Paris himself that spring, a man of thirty-three or so, feeling as old almost as he did today, a widower with his little girl. If only they might have met then, he and that serious, starry-eyed girl in the photograph!

Hearing Pete coming, he set the photograph back in its place, and, sitting down, picked up the first paper within reach.

"Good night, sir," said Pete from the doorway.

"Good night, my dear boy. Good luck!" They shook hands.

"Funny old duck," Pete thought as he went down-stairs whistling, "sitting there so contentedly reading 'The Harvard Lampoon.' Wonder what he thinks of it."

He did not wonder long, though, for more interesting subjects of consideration were at hand. What reception would he meet at the Farrons? What arrangements would be made, what assumptions permitted? But even more immediate than this was the problem how could he contrive to greet Mrs. Farron? He was shocked to find how little he had been able to forgive her. There was something devilish, he thought, in the way she had contrived to shake his self-confidence at the moment of all others when he had needed it. He could never forget a certain contemptuous curve in her fine, clear profile or the smooth delight of her tone at some of her own cruelties. Some day he would have it out with her when the right moment came. Before he reached the house he had had time to sketch a number of scenes in which she, caught extraordinarily red-handed, was forced to listen to his exposition of the evil of such methods as hers. He would say to her, "I remember that you once said to me, Mrs. Farron -" Anger cut short his vision as a cloud of her phrases came back to him, like stinging bees.

He had hoped for a minute alone with Mathilde, but as Pringle opened the drawing-room door for him he heard the sound of laughter, and seeing that even Mrs. Farron herself was down, he exclaimed quickly:

"What, am I late?"

Every one laughed all the more at this.

"That's just what Mr. Farron said you would say at finding that Mama was dressed in time," exclaimed Mathilde, casting an admiring glance at her stepfather.

" You'd suppose I'd never been in time for dinner

before," remarked Adelaide, giving Wayne her long hand.

"But isn't it wonderful, Pete," put in Mathilde, "how Mr. Farron is always right?"

"Oh, I hope he isn't," said Adelaide; "for what do you think he has just been telling me - that you'd always hate me, Pete, as long as you lived. You see," she went on, the little knot coming in her eyebrows, "I've been telling him all the things I said to you yesterday. They did sound rather awful, and I think I've forgotten some of the worst."

"*I* haven't," said Pete.

"I remember I told you you were no one."

"You said I was a perfectly nice young man."

"And that you had no business judgment."

"And that I was mixing Mathilde up with a fraud."

"And that I couldn't see any particular reason why she cared about you."

"That you only asked that your son-in-law should be a person."

"I am afraid I said something about not coming to a house where you weren't welcome."

"I know you said something about a bribe."

At this Adelaide laughed out loud.

Alice Duer Miller

"I believe I did," she said. "What things one does say sometimes! There's dinner." She rose, and tucked her hand under his arm. "Will you take me in to dinner, Pete, or do you think I'm too despicable to be fed?"

The truth was that they were all four in such high spirits that they could no more help playing together than four colts could help playing in a grass field. Besides, Vincent had taunted Adelaide with her inability ever to make it up with Wayne. She left no trick unturned.

"I don't know," she went on as they sat down at table, "that a marriage is quite legal unless you hate your mother-in-law. I ought to give you some opportunity to go home and say to Mrs. Wayne, 'But I'm afraid I shall never be able to get on with Mrs. Farron.'"

"Oh, he's said that already," remarked Vincent.

"Many a time," said Pete.

Mathilde glanced a little fearfully at her mother. The talk seemed to her amusing, but dangerous.

"Well, then, shall we have a feud, Pete?" said Adelaide in a glass-of-wine-with-you-sir tone. "A good feud in a family can be made very amusing."

"It would be all right for us, of course," said Pete, "but it would be rather hard on Mathilde."

"Mathilde is a better fighter than either of you," put in Vincent. "Adelaide has no continuity of purpose, and you, Pete, are wretchedly kind-hearted; but Mathilde would go into it to the death."

"Oh, I don't know what you mean, Mr. Farron," exclaimed Mathilde, tremendously flattered, and hoping he would go on. "I don't like to fight."

"Neither did Stonewall Jackson, I believe, until they fixed bayonets."

Mathilde, dropping her eyes, saw Pete's hand lying on the table. It was stubby, and she loved it the better for being so; it was firm and boyish and exactly like Pete. Looking up, she caught her mother's eye, and they both remembered. For an instant indecision flickered in Adelaide's look, but she lacked the complete courage to add that to the list - to tell any human being that she had said his hands were stubby; and so her eyes fell before her daughter's.

As dinner went on the adjustment between the four became more nearly perfect; the gaiety, directed by Adelaide, lost all sting. But even as she talked to Pete she was only dimly aware of his existence. Her audience was her husband. She was playing for his praise and admiration, and before soup was over she knew she had it; she knew better than words could tell her that he thought her the most desirable woman in the world. Fortified by that knowledge, the pacification of a cross boy seemed to Adelaide an inconsiderable task.

By the time they rose from table it was accomplished. As they went into the drawing-room Adelaide was thinking that young men were really rather geese, but, then, one wouldn't have them different if one could.

Vincent was thinking how completely attaching a nature like hers would always be to him, since when

Alice Duer Miller

she yielded her will to his she did it with such complete generosity.

Mathilde was saying to herself:

"Of course I knew Pete's charm would win Mama at last, but even I did not suppose he could do it the very first evening."

And Pete was thinking:

"A former beauty thinks she can put anything over, and in a way she can. I feel rather friendly toward her."

The Farrons had decided while they were dressing that after dinner they would retire to Vincent's study and give the lovers a few minutes to themselves.

Left alone, Pete and Mathilde stood looking seriously at each other, and then at the room which only a few weeks before had witnessed their first prolonged talk.

"I never saw your mother look a quarter as beautiful as she does this evening," said Wayne.

"Isn't she marvelous, the way she can make up for everything when she wants?" Mathilde answered with enthusiasm.

Pete shook his head.

"She can never make up for one thing."

"O Pete!"

" She can never give me back my first instinctive,

egotistical, divine conviction that there was every reason why you should love me. I shall always hear her voice saying, 'But why should Mathilde love you?' And I shall never know a good answer."

"What," cried Mathilde, "don't you know the answer to that! I do. Mama doesn't, of course. Mama loves people for reasons outside themselves: she loves me because I'm her child, and Grandpapa because he's her father, and Mr. Farron because she thinks he's strong. If she didn't think him strong, I'm not sure she'd love him. But *I* love *you* for being just as you are, because you are my choice. Whatever you do or say, that can't be changed -"

The door opened, and Pringle entered with a tray in his hand, and his eyes began darting about in search of empty coffee-cups. Mathilde and Pete were aware of a common feeling of guilt, not that they were concealing the cups, though there was something of that accusation in Pringle's expression, but because the pause between them was so obvious. So Mathilde said suddenly:

"Pringle, Mr. Wayne and I are engaged to be married."

"Indeed, Miss?" said Pringle, with a smile; and so seldom was this phenomenon seen to take place that Wayne noted for the first time that Pringle's teeth were false. "I'm delighted to hear it; and you, too, sir. This is a bad world to go through alone."

"Do you approve of marriage, Pringle?" said Wayne.

The cups, revealing themselves one by one, were secured as Pringle answered:

Alice Duer Miller

"In my class of life, sir, we don't give much time to considering what we approve of and disapprove of. But young people are all alike when they're first engaged, always wondering how it is going to turn out, and hoping the other party won't know that they're wondering. But when you get old, and you look back on all the mistakes and the disadvantages and the sacrifices, you'll find that you won't be able to imagine that you could have gone through it with any other person - in spite of her faults," he added almost to himself.

When he was gone, Pete and Mathilde turned and kissed each other.

"When we get old -" they murmured.

They really believed that it could never happen to them.

www.ingramcontent.com/pod-product-compliance
Lightning Source LLC
Chambersburg PA
CBHW030112180626
46812CB00002B/385